Palermo

A Place To Die

By Jerry Bader
Illustrations by Paola Ceccantoni

MRPwebmedia.com/books

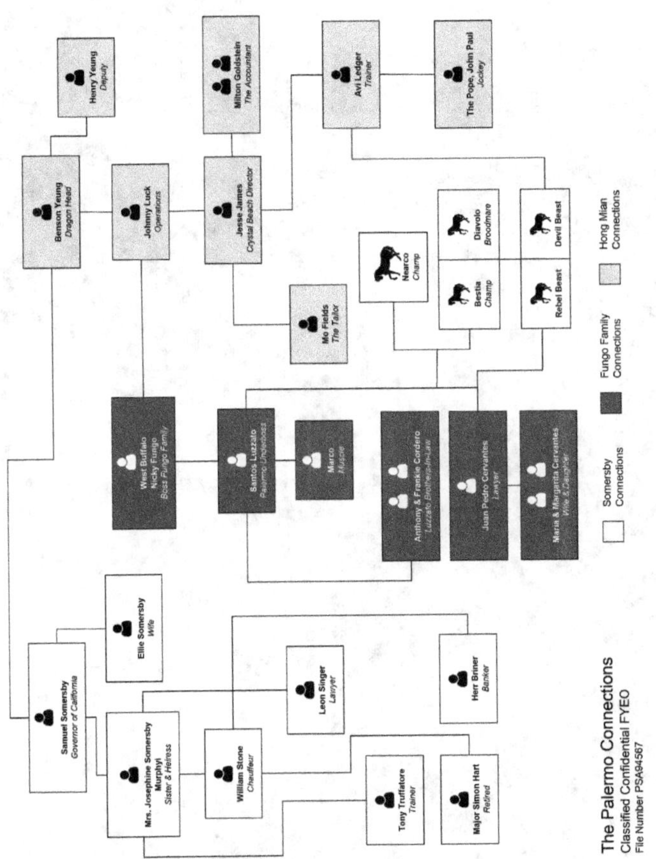

THE PALERMO CONNECTIONS

BESTIA'S LAST STAND

Part One

1
Bestia's Last Stand

It's dawn, an unsettling time, not quite day and not quite night; a time of promise for some and dread for others. The merchants and residents had been warned to stay off the street; they needn't be told what would happen if they didn't.

The early morning light begins to reveal the muted ochre and brown stucco painted buildings with their ornate wrought-iron balconies fronting the chocolate-colored shutters that hang over the ancient narrow cobblestone streets. The door to the Osteria opens just a crack. Owner Federico Falcone, quickly sneaks out to bring in the several large white clay flowerpots that guard his front entrance. He's replaced the damn trees several times already this year. Enough is enough. If the Mafia bandits that sponsor this circus want to murder him for protecting his beloved trees, so be it, but he's sick and tired of the young punks that lose their wages on the race, taking it out on his trees... fuck them.

The picture postcard scene belies the brutal carnage that is about to start. Middle-aged men with pockets stuffed with cash to bet gather along the street; young men on Vespa motor scooters rev their engines while they trade macho insults punctuated by hand gestures exclusive to Sicilian conversation. The crowd stands ready to alternatively condemn and cajole their favorite while taunting and harassing the others; old men put out folding chairs on the balconies that hang only a few feet above the mayhem that is about to take place below. Today is race day in Monreale on the outskirts of Palermo, Sicily.

But these aren't your ordinary civilized legal horse races on manicured tracks with qualified stewards, licensed veterinarians, and professional jockeys; these are Mafia-backed street races, without rules, regulations, or protections. This is a blood sport in its most cruel and sadistic incarnation. The course is a four hundred meter sprint along the Via Odigitria from Via Torres to the bistro where Odigitria makes an abrupt right turn into Via Ritito and the flower shop that divides it into two separate unequal portions.

Odigitria is hardly wide enough to accommodate the four horses entered. The word that Bestia is running, perhaps for the last time, spread through the region like an announcement of free cash. His presence meant bigger crowds, more money, and added excitement. Bestia guaranteed a huge payday for the gangsters, maybe as much as fifty or sixty thousand Euros for the one race. The champ was still money in the bank despite his poor condition: the result of prolonged abuse. The animal's raw athletic power was gone, but the spirit was still intact.

As a two-year-old Bestia won both the Premio Primi Passi and the Gran Criterium, both held in Milan. As a three-year-old it won the Derby Italiano, the Premio Federico Tesio, and the Premio Roma. After winning the Roma, the colt was sold to a syndicate run by Santos Luzzato, nephew to Nicky The Mushroom Fungo, newly appointed boss of the Buffalo Fungo Crime Family. Santos had aspirations of joining his Uncle in the States; he obviously never had the pleasure of visiting western New York's Queen City.

Santos intended to parlay his illegal street racing money machine and back-barn breeding experience into a venture that fed his Uncle yearlings that could be sold to American stables and novice owners looking to cash-in on European thoroughbreds with seemingly attractive pedigrees. Bestia was supposed to be the foundation of this horse breeding empire, but the champ was unenthusiastic.

Bestia might have been a winner on the racetrack, but when it came to the ladies, he was either uninterested or particularly picky. After an infuriating number of false starts, Bestia finally found a broodmare, Diavolo, to his liking. The pair threw-off a couple of colts: one was an impressive black beauty, Rebel Beast, a monster standing eighteen hands high, a carbon copy in looks to its sire. The other, Devil Beast, a runt, was a less than inspiring shabby looking Bay, stretching to a mere fifteen hands high. Devil Beast was sold off to an Argentinean lawyer for a modest sum while Rebel Beast was kept for development.

Unfortunately Rebel Beast turned out to be more trouble than it was worth. The horse was perpetually fractious, unwilling to co-operate with trainers, grooms, jockeys, veterinarians, or anyone that tried to get near it. Eventually Rebel Beast was sent to Luzzato's brother-in-laws in California, the Cordero brothers. Anthony and Frankie Cordero who with Luzzato's help opened a fledgling horse operation on the outskirts of Anaheim. The Corderos sold the troubled three-year-old to Mrs. Josephine Somersby Murphy, a billionaire peanut butter heiress and sister of California Governor Samuel Somersby.

There is little sentiment in the legitimate horse racing business, so it is not surprising that the illegal side of things is downright cold-blooded. Caring for a horse is expensive; it cost the equivalent of two thousand dollars a month to keep a horse, and not even a champion like Bestia was worth the investment if it couldn't pay its way. That meant Bestia would be shot, carved up, and sold to a local Macelleria, a butcher shop, or put on the street racing circuit. One way or another, Bestia was going to pay for itself.

Today the champ is the prohibitive favorite. It was Bestia's last chance to avoid the butcher's cleaver, but Santos Luzzato doesn't rely on chance, and a Bestia win would not maximize the desired financial return. Luzzato gives three of the four jockeys their final instructions. "Do whatever you got to do, but Bestia can't win."

He leaves the jockeys and returns to his red Ferrari. He starts the engine and races down Odigitria to the bistro where he makes the hard right parking in front of the flower shop that abruptly dissects Via Ritito. He joins the crowd that's gathered at the bistro. As he approaches three different tables of men stand giving him the choice of locations to view the finish of the race. Mafiosi have their privileges.

The horses lineup on Via Odigitria across from the church. The anticipation of the race and the possibility of seeing Bestia run for the last time has created added excitement and increased betting. The crowd overflows into the street where the horses are about to run. The men yell instructions to the jockeys, demanding they prove their worth, while the punks on the scooters rev their engines and hurl *vaffanculo* insults at each other.

One of Luzzato's men fires a pistol in the air and the race begins. Unlike the orderly start of a legitimate horserace, this is chaos. The four horses race down Odigitria with the punks on scooters chasing them as they scream insults and encouragements at the riders. It's closer to Circus Maximus than Churchill Downs.

The horses pound down the cobblestones with the jockeys bumping each other in an effort to throw each other off stride, Bestia is the main target as per Luzzato's instructions, but the horse's will is too strong. Bestia fights off the pretenders with his guts while his jockey uses his whip on the heads and arms of the opponents trying to box him in. The bistro's in sight, and Bestia has taken the lead; but strong as he is, the years have taken their toll. One of the other horses has caught up, but Bestia is still in the lead by a head when the second horse violently lugs-in, driving Bestia into the crowd gathered at the bistro. As the people scatter, Bestia and his rider go headlong through the window of the tavern as Luzzato and the assembled men watched in horror.

WHERE HAVE YOU GONE MRS. MURPHY?

2
Where Have You Gone Mrs. Murphy?

You reach a certain age and visits to the doctor become a regular occurrence. Today is Mrs. Josephine Somersby Murphy's semi-annual checkup, and it comes none too soon. For the average working-class American, a doctor's visit is a choice between good health and eating, but this isn't the case for Mrs. Murphy. When your late husband dies from boardroom stress leaving you one-point-seven-billion dollars in peanut butter common stock and sundry other securities, you'd think money was the last thing on your mind, but the more you have, the more you obsess over losing it. It's not easy to lose that kind of money, but it can be done if you try hard enough.

Mrs. Murphy was not in any danger of losing her outlandish fortune; horse racing was merely an expensive hobby; it gives her something to do between meetings with her broker, and besides; it provides entrée into the sporty horsey set, where money, lots of money, was just so ordinary; society success required stake winners, and if the Derby found its way onto your resume all the better. Murphy had her share of stake winners, but to date, the Derby has eluded her.

Horse racing is not a sport for the meek or faint of heart. No matter how much money you throw at the sport, it wants more. Sometimes things go

right, but more often than not, they don't. For
Murphy, there was the loss of the beautiful spirit
horse, Medicine Hat; the murder of her trainer,
Danny O'Conner, up in Canada; and the disaster
in Florida. And now, god-damn-it, there was the
scam inflicted by those conmen, the Cordero
brothers, who sold her that nut case, Rebel Beast.

The Italian-bred beauty had a pedigree that went
all the way back to Nearco, and it definitely
looked the part, standing eighteen hands high
with a glistening black coat. He sure as hell
looked like the million dollars she laid out to buy
him. But this horse was crazy.

Her trainer, Tony Truffatore, warned her, but she
didn't listen. Nearco for Christ's sake, that was
the kind of pedigree that owners drool over, but
Rebel Beast was wacky. None of the jockeys
would take the mount; he was just too
dangerous. He'd flip and kick and bite; no one
could get near him unless he was tranquilized.
Murphy already lost two grooms and Truffatore
was demanding that she get rid of him or he'd
quit. It wasn't the million dollars that was
causing her stress, as much as the loss of respect
and reputation amongst her social peers.

She'd already spoken to her lawyers about suing
the sons-of-bitches that sold her the beast, but
the Corderos put the blame on the breeder, some
Italian named Santos Luzzato. As far as the
Corderos were concerned it was a case of buyer

beware; she bought the horse as is, no guarantees.

After her doctor's visit, she and her chauffeur, William Stone, would be on their way to Rome for a few days relaxation; and then on to Palermo, Sicily where she intended to track down this Luzzato fellow who bred the incorrigible animal. She'd find out the real story behind this horse, and if things weren't kosher, she'd cause a stink, after all, she's not only rich, she's the Governor's sister.

Maybe Doctor Kennedy could give her something that would relax her on the flight over. That's really what she needed, something to take the edge off. When Murphy enters the doctor's office she is immediately ushered into an examining room where Doctor Kennedy is waiting. After a thorough examination he pronounces her fit as a fiddle, except for the slightly higher than normal blood pressure that both doctor and patient attribute to the whole Rebel Beast situation.

Kennedy, as always, is sympathetic. He suggests an injection of something new designed to calm the most-jagged nerves. Murphy agrees without bothering to question what he's giving her, but whatever it is, it certainly does the trick. Murphy tries to stand but falls back into the chair.

Kennedy calls his nurse who brings a wheel chair and William, the chauffeur. As William wheels his boss out, the doctor assures his patient that the effects will wear-off before they land at Rome's Fiumicino Airport.

On the way down to the parking garage, Mrs. Murphy attempts to text her trainer, Tony Truffatore, with the address of where she's staying in Sicily, but she's confused and more than a bit groggy. All she manages to type is the single word, "Palermo" before William notices.

"You don't want to be texting in your condition." He attempts to grab the phone out of her hands; she resists, accidentally hitting the send button. "See…" says William as he grabs the phone. "You can have your phone back when you're feeling yourself."

SO LONG, IT'S BEEN GOOD TO KNOW YOU

3
So Long, It's Been Good To Know You

When Tony Truffatore got the one word text, "Palermo," from Mrs. Murphy he thought it was strange, but ultimately he assumed it was just a mistake. The second message he received made more sense, Murphy made a deal with Luzzato to have the Cordero brothers unload the troubled horse to a numbered company in Argentina. The Corderos were to send a crew to pick up the horse and have it shipped to Buenos Aires, Palermo, Argentina.

That seemed to answer the trainer's concern over the original one word text; however, the timing did seem a little strange. Of course you can use your mobile phone to text while in the air, but still, negotiating a contract while flying over the Atlantic with someone who just screwed you, seemed a bit out of character for the wily peanut butter heiress. But really, who gives a rat's ass, as long as the deal was done. Her lawyer must have handled the details. In the end he didn't care how she did it, as long as he was rid of the truculent beast.

Truffatore stood staring at Rebel Beast in his stall; the horse stared right back as if to say: *'You want some of this, asshole... come a little closer and we'll see what you got.'* Truffatore just shook his head in response to the horse's silent taunt. The crazy bastard was someone else's problem now, and that was a blessing. Things were moving quickly; the trailer picking up the horse was pulling into shed row. It didn't look like they sent a vet to give the horse something to calm it down for transport. Why make things easy?

Two Mexican grooms get out of the truck and approach Truffatore. There are documents that need to be signed. Truffatore wants to make sure nothing goes wrong. They go into his small shed row office and sign a bunch of papers. The men proceed to take Rebel Beast out of its stall and lead him to where the trailer is parked. For some strange reason the horse is co-operative.

Truffatore can't believe it. He stands there with his hands on his hips watching in amazement, but true to form, Rebel Beast is just playing possum.

One of the men positions the ramp into the trailer while the other man tries to lead the horse up the incline, but Rebel Beast just stops. The second man goes behind the horse to try to push him, but Rebel Beast kicks wildly barely missing the Mexican groom. The more they try, the wilder Rebel Beast gets, within a few minutes the horse is snarling, snorting, and rearing back on its hind legs. The Mexicans have lost control. They finally get the horse calmed down, but he's not moving anywhere. He just stands at the edge of the ramp defying the two men to try to get him in the trailer.

Truffatore figures if he doesn't help, he'll never get this nut case out of his life, and all the commotion is upsetting the other horses. He goes into his office and calls Doc Simons, his vet, asking him to come right over. Truffatore grabs a big towel that is hanging on a hook on the back of his door. He takes it to the two grooms. The towel is placed over Rebel Beast's head in an effort to calm the horse down. If they can just keep the horse quiet till Doc Simons arrives with some ACE (Acepromazine), the problem should be resolved.

ACE isn't the best solution for calming an agitated horse, but thoroughbreds can be dangerous when they get upset. Not only are they a potential danger to their handlers; they can be a danger to themselves. Rebel Beast wouldn't be the first horse that had to be put down because he injured himself while in an overly agitated state.

ACE usually calms a horse down but it can have multiple side effects, including acting as a muscle relaxant, which sounds harmless enough until you understand that it can cause a colt like Rebel Beast to 'drop' its penis, and in extreme cases can cause paralysis, gangrene, and eventual amputation. Not a pleasant thought.

Truffatore volunteers to pay to have the horse tranquilized since the two Mexicans only have about twelve dollars between them, and neither one speaks more than six words of English. He didn't care about the money; he just wanted to get Rebel Beast out of his barn as quickly as possible, besides: he'd charge Murphy three times over for Doc Simon's visit.

The veterinarian arrives and gives Rebel Beast the shot. The horse calms down enough that the two grooms with the help of Truffatore and Simons are able to get him in the trailer and on his way to sunny Argentina, at least, that was the plan.

As the Mexicans barrel down the highway with Rebel Beast in tow they are t-boned by an empty produce truck on its way to pick up a load of walnuts. The grooms end up in the hospital with multiple lacerations, groggy, and in shock, but essentially unharmed. Rebel Beast is not so lucky.

The trailer is hit broadside, killing Rebel Beast instantly. The driver of the truck somehow disappears from the scene without a trace. One of the Mexicans has a hazy recollection of seeing a car pick up the truck driver shortly after the accident before the police and ambulance arrive.

There are no other witnesses to the event. When the Mexicans are released from the hospital, they are immediately turned over to ICE (Immigration and Customs Enforcement) agents who deport the pair within hours. All very nice and neat, too neat from Truffatore's standpoint, but then, that's the horse racing business. The Argentinean numbered company was inline to collect the two-million-dollar accidental death insurance policy that clicked-in on taking possession of the horse, very convenient.

Truffatore smelled a rat, but he's been around long enough to know when to mind his own business. Whether it was the Cordero brothers who owned the Argentinean shell company, the Italian breeder, Luzzato, or Mrs. Murphy herself, it really didn't matter, as long as he wasn't responsible for the horse.

The fact that somebody made a pile of dough from the death of Rebel Beast was none of Truffatore's business, not yet at least, but that was about to change.

THE NEGOTIATION

4
The Negotiation

It's a beautiful Sicilian morning and Mrs. Josephine Murphy, heiress, thoroughbred racehorse owner, and sister of the Governor of California is enjoying her sumptuous Italian breakfast on the patio of the five-star Grand Hotel Villa Igiea Palermo. Her chauffeur, William Stone, was out renting a car for her to take to Monreale where she arranged to have dinner with Santos Luzzato to discuss the purchase of several juvenile horses. On the phone she flattered Luzzato with praise for his reputation as Sicily's finest breeder of thoroughbred racehorses. Nonsense of course, but seemingly effective as he seemed anxious to meet and discuss a deal for new horses. She played the rich, dumb, bitch card to the hilt, but once she had him in her sights, she'd bring down the hammer of a stinking rich heiress with teams of lawyers and a brother who was Governor of California.

She wanted compensation for Rebel Beast and she was determined to get it. She didn't care that her white-shoe lawyers warned her he was related to Nicky Fungo. So what if he had the reputation as a treacherous Mafia son-of-a-bitch? When it came to sons-of-bitches, she felt she could hold her own. Besides, what was he going to do, shoot her in the middle of the Ristorante Bacco dining room? Once William delivered the renter, he could have the rest of the day off to see the sights of Palermo or whatever chauffeurs do when they have some free time.

The drive from Palermo to Monreale was uneventful. She only managed to get lost twice which she deemed a victory. When she met Santos Luzzato in the lobby of the Ristorante Bacco at the appointed time, she was pleasantly surprised. For some silly reason she'd pictured an old school, middle-aged Mafioso with a pencil-thin moustache and slick-backed hair wearing a chalk-striped three-piece suit and pointed shoes. In fact Santos Luzzato was a clean-shaven, handsome, thirty-something gentleman wearing a Brioni wool and silk blend suit and Gucci loafers with an open-neck white custom Egyptian cotton shirt. His English was flawless with a slight Italian accent that would sweep just about any North American widow off her feet. He insisted on having one of his men take her car to a safe parking area because you just couldn't leave expensive automobiles unattended on the street.

Even dinner turned out to be a pleasant surprise. He ordered the best wine on the menu and two perfectly prepared Argentine steaks, pasta, and grilled peppers. For dessert there was the most exquisite chocolate encrusted vanilla tartufo with the best coffee she ever had. When the conversation turned to the business of horses, he was very understanding. He knew Rebel Beast was a problem horse but his American brothers-in-law wanted him for stud, or so they said. He resisted, but his wife was insistent, her brothers wanted to start a horse breeding business and they needed a sire with a good pedigree.

He had no idea they sold the horse, and he was mortified that his relatives unloaded the troubled thoroughbred to such an elegant and delightful woman as Mrs. Murphy. He promised compensation in the form of two juvenile thoroughbreds that would more than make up for Rebel Beast. All she had to do was sign over Rebel Beast to him and he would replace the animal with two beautiful juveniles that would more than make up for her trouble. He was so eager to please that he called his lawyer immediately to prepare the documents and bring them over to the restaurant while they finished their meal. Tomorrow he would meet her in Palermo with the documents for the two replacement horses. He would arrange transportation and hopefully this would be a long and prosperous relationship for both parties. As far as the Cordero brothers were concerned, he would deal with them. All in all, the meeting was a triumph of reasonable quality people who understood how the rich do business. All that Mafia talk from her lawyers was just silly; the man was a gent.

Luzzato pays the bill and accompanies Mrs. Murphy to her car. The Alfa Romeo Brera is parked right in front of the restaurant with one of Luzzato's men standing guard. Murphy is so pleased with her successful meeting, and the charm of the Italian dreamboat, that she doesn't notice the grease stain on the shirt sleeve of Luzzato's man, nor does she see the heavy wire cutters causing the man's suit pocket to bulge. Luzzato is kind enough to suggest a picturesque route through the mountains back to Palermo. Tomorrow he'll meet Murphy at her hotel for lunch and deliver the documents for the two juveniles. Murphy heads back to Palermo. While driving out of town, she texts William Stone, her chauffeur, about Luzzato's offer of compensation. Stone not only functions as her chauffeur, he also acts as her executive assistant.

In the morning two hikers find Murphy's car. It went off the mountain highway at a notorious hairpin turn that was literally impossible to navigate unless you knew it was coming. When the police arrive, the crime scene techs notice the brake lines on the upside down Alfa Romeo had been cut, but they're told to leave that detail out of their report. Mrs. Murphy's body is found twenty yards down the mountain. She wasn't wearing her seat belt causing her to be propelled through the windshield. She came to a dead stop when her head hit the trunk of a Sicilian Fir tree.

WE REGRETFULLY INFORM YOU…

5
We Regretfully Inform You of The Passing of...

Truffatore wakes from the best night's sleep he's had since that crazy Rebel Beast arrived in his barn. Thank God that was over, now he could get back to training Murphy's other horses. He swings his legs over the side of the bed, his feet finding the soft grey carpet of his rented three-bedroom PUD-style home in the gated Bellagio Court community of Arcadia, California. Life is good and the new condo is only a twenty-minute drive to the Hancock Racetrack. He sits for a minute getting his bearings. He read somewhere that you should never just jump out of bed; it can cause a heart attack. It's most likely bullshit, besides he's already survived threats from Nicky The Mushroom Fungo and his Hong Mian counterpart Johnny Luck. If those two *stronzi* didn't give him a heart attack, it was unlikely getting out of bed too fast would do the trick, but why take the chance.

Slow and easy is the way to start your day. He looked forward to his morning newspaper, coffee, and egg white omelet; perhaps he'd celebrate today with breakfast at the State Diner and indulge in one of Carman's humongous muffins. Carman and her goofy Chinese husband run the State Diner. It serves as a morning meeting place for trainers, jockeys, and track people in the area. With Carman, you never knew what kind of muffin you're going to get, no matter what you ordered, or what was on special. You just took what Carman gave you and told her it was great, because it usually was.

Rumor is, Carman and her husband Barney were connected; the giveaway is the Guan Yu pin Barney insists on wearing on his chocolate, blueberry, and grease-stained white shirt. And then there's Carman's cousin Arlo, who seems to be perpetually sleeping in the corner. Some say he's there as protection, just in case someone gets out of hand because they were served a banana muffin instead of a chocolate. You just didn't mess with Carman. Truffatore showered, dressed, and headed for the State Diner where he hoped to enjoy a peaceful, uneventful breakfast. Life was good.

Truffatore parks his car in front of the long silver tube with the exposed rivets that is the State Diner. One look and you know this place is a relic of the Rosie The Riveter era: a place with huge muffins, jukeboxes, cheap prices, and more than its share of entertaining waitress banter.

Truffatore gets out of his car and stops dead in his tracks. His appetite suddenly disappears. A cold sweat starts to form between the raised-hairs on the back of his neck. He feels the bile rising up from his stomach into his mouth. The headline in the LA Times prominently displayed in the ancient newspaper box screams out in heavy forty-eight-point bold Belizio, "Governor's Sister Killed In Sicily."

Truffatore takes out his phone and taps on the number for the Shanghai Player's Club. A woman answers, "Shanghai Player's Club, Mr. Luck's office."

"Tell him Tony Trufffatore has to see him right away."

"Can I tell him what it's concerning,"

"Yeah sure... tell him to check out the morning edition of the LA Times."

JESSE'S BACK IN TOWN

6

Jesse's Back In Town

Truffatore drives directly to the Shanghai Player's Club where he is immediately ushered into a boardroom by Luck's beautiful young Chinese executive assistant. Truffatore's shoes sink deep into the high-pile charcoal grey hand-knotted Chinese rug. The secretary tells Truffatore to take a seat while he waits for Mr. Luck to arrive. Within minutes she brings him a freshly brewed carafe of coffee along with three cups, cream, sugar, and a plate piled high with multicolored Macarons made in the club's dining room kitchen. He gladly accepts the coffee and cookies. The room is dominated by a long black-lacquer Parson's table surrounded by twelve high-backed soft as butter leather chairs; half the chairs face a giant sixty-inch flat screen television. The other six chairs face two priceless Chinese scrolls of wild horses that bracket the expansive picture window that overlooks the racetrack.

The Shanghai Player's Club is part of the Hancock Entertainment Complex consisting of the members only Shanghai Player's Club, the Hancock Casino, the Hancock Racetrack, the Starting Gate Saloon, and the newly opened Hancock Towers, a luxury hotel, with condo residences, a live performance theater, and a shopping mall with the finest shops from around the world. The place is operated by a consortium of interests that include: the Hong Mian Investment Corporation, Fungo Enterprises, and a syndicate of Native American interests that hold the operating license for the Hancock Casino. Johnny Luck represents the Hong Mian and is President of the whole operation although other executives and employees come from each of the various investment groups.

After about fifteen minutes Luck arrives holding a copy of the LA Times. He's followed into the room by an attractive young blonde, Jesse James. Jesse is an ex-jockey and Hong Mian executive despite the fact she's not Chinese. After Jesse's father died, Luck took her in and raised her to follow in his footsteps. For the last couple of years, Jesse was up in Canada running a couple of racetracks for the Hong Mian. Now, she's back in LA as Vice President of Operations and Director of the Hancock Racetrack, not bad for a barely thirty-year-old orphan and daughter of a white trash criminal rug salesman. Truffatore knows Jesse. She was neck deep in that whole Florida business that made headlines around the world. He knows that for a fact because he was involved as well. Jesse is as tough as she is attractive. Rumor has it, she never goes anywhere without her pearl-handled switchblade. The girl is dangerous and smart.

They each pour a cup of coffee and take their seats. Luck throws the newspaper in the middle of the table. He looks at Truffatore, and speaks, "So?"

Truffatore: "She's dead!"

"I can see that. It says it right here," Luck jabs a finger at the headline in the paper, "… in forty-eight point black type."

Truffatore: "She's been murdered."

"Really?" Says Jesse. "You mean someone beat us to the punch?"

Truffatore: "Seriously, there's more to this than her just going off the road in the Sicilian mountains."

Luck: "What the hell was she doing in Sicily?"

Truffatore: "She was trying to get her money back on a horse deal that went bad."

Jesse: "What horse deal?"

Truffatore: "She bought a three-year-old, Rebel Beast, from a couple of Italian shysters, the Cordero Brothers. The horse was impossible. Nobody could ride him, so these brothers tell her buyer-beware; take it up with the breeder, some Sicilian named Luzzato. Next thing I know she's on a plane to Sicily and I get a text message telling me she had the Corderos unload the horse to some Argentinean company."

Jesse: "That's not the horse that was killed in a truck accident, is it?"

Truffatore: "Yeah that's the one. I knew something was wrong right from the get-go."

Luck: "How's that?"

Truffatore, "Before her plane even left the ground, I got a one word text, 'Palermo.' Then nothing until the text about the sale to the Argentinean outfit. I think the brothers or this Luzzato guy had her killed."

Jesse: "Why?"

Truffatore: "Rebel Beast was insured for two million bucks."

Jesse: "Horse deals go bad all the time. You just right it off and move on for Christ's sake, the woman had more money than God."

Truffatore: "It doesn't matter how much dough they got, they beat her for a million bucks, and she was determined to be compensated. I warned her about the Corderos."

Luck: "So what's this got to do with us?"

Truffatore: "Aren't you guys involved with Somersby? Didn't he approve the deal with the Indians for the casino? He's not going to be happy that his sister gets bumped off by your partners."

Luck: "What do you mean, our partners?"

Truffatore: "This whole thing smells like 'mushrooms' if you catch my drift?" Luck and Jesse look concerned. "Maybe you should give your Buffalo pal a call and see what he knows about this. I'm doing you a favor here. There seems to be a whole lot of Sicilian horse racing people involved. Somersby goes on the warpath thinking you guys killed his sister, it could be big trouble for everybody."

Luck: "I'll check it out. Just leave it with us, and if you hear anything else, let us know."

Truffatore: "Somebody is going to inherit a shit-pile of peanut butter stock, as well as her horses. Plus, people like Murphy usually have an insurance policy with lots of zeros." Traffatore says his goodbyes and leaves.

Luck turns to Jesse, "I'll call Nicky and find out if he knows anything about these Cordero brothers. In the meantime why don't you pay them a visit and take the Tailor with you."

Jesse: "I can handle it myself. Why bother Mo with this thing?"

Luck: "Take the Tailor. If these guys had their Sicilian relatives kill Murphy, they're not going to think twice about dusting you in their doorway. Just take Mo for backup."

THE CORDERO CONFRONTATION

7

The Cordero Confrontation

Jesse and Mo Fields, The Tailor, make the hour and forty minute drive to the Cordero Thoroughbred Horse Farm on the outskirts of Anaheim in an hour and fifteen minutes with Jesse pushing her black convertible Audi TT to its limit. The facility is enclosed behind a black wrought iron gate with a galloping thoroughbred acting as the handle. A white painted wooden booth stands at the side of the gate with a young man in jeans, cowboy shirt and pistol slung from his hips like Wyatt Earp sitting listening to the Angels' baseball game. He approaches the Audi.

"Can I help you?"

Jesse gives the young cowboy a big smile. Mo Fields gets out of the car as if to stretch his legs. "We're here to speak to the brothers."

"I'll check the list. What's your name?" The guard goes back to the booth and reaches for a clipboard that rests on a counter beside the radio playing the ball game. He looks up at Mo who is standing right beside him, "Name?"

"Tom Mix…"

The young guard runs his finger up and down the list a couple of times. He places the clipboard back on the counter. "I don't see it on the list. If you're not on the list, I can't let you in."

"There it is," says Mo, as he points to a random name on the list.

The cowboy lowers his head to look closer at where Mo is pointing, "That doesn't say Tom…" but before the cowboy can finish Mo Fields slams his head into the counter knocking him out cold. He turns to Jesse who's out of her car opening the gate. She throws him a roll of three-inch grey duck tape. It takes Fields only a few minutes to bind the cowboy's feet and hands so he can't move. He rips one last piece of tape and places it over the young man's mouth. He props the unconscious cowboy up on his stool so he can listen to the game when he comes to. Mo takes a white linen hanky out of his pocket and uses it to remove the cowboy's gun from its holster. He unloads the pistol careful not to get his fingerprints on the gun. He puts the bullets in the pocket of his suit jacket and replaces the gun back into its holster.

Mo gets back into the Audi and Jesse drives up to the large well-manicured house that functions as the Cordero brothers' office and residence. They park in the circular driveway and walk up to the front door and ring the bell. A few minutes later a middle-aged Hispanic woman comes to the door, "Puedo ayudarte por favor"

Jesse answers, "Sí, por favor, me gusta hablar con los hermanos." The woman goes away and in a few minutes a handsome thirty-something man in jeans and a work shirt comes to the door. He is Anthony Cordero. He looks at the pretty blonde and the well-dressed man standing off to the side with his hands behind his back.

 "Who the hell are you two and how did you get in here?"

Jesse smiles, "We came for the money."

Anthony: "What the hell kind of Mormons are you? You don't even offer a pamphlet?"

Jesse: "Do we look like Mormons to you, asshole? Besides... they don't take your dough right off; first they save your worthless soul, then they take your money."

Anthony: "Who the fuck are you?"

Jesse smiles her big smile. "We're the guys who came to collect the refund on the money you swindled from Josephine Murphy."

Anthony: "First of all we didn't swindle that old broad. Murphy knows the score, you buy it; you own it; that's the deal. She's no rookie, she knows the score."

Jesse: "Actually she knows nothing, cause she's dead. Currently she's laid out on a metal table covered with a white sheet in a morgue in Sicily."

Anthony: "Tough break for the old battle axe, but that's got nothing to do with us, besides, who the hell sends a little girl and her daddy to collect?"

Jesse: "You really don't want to know, so just give us the fucking money."

By this time the other Cordero brother, Frankie, has come to the door. He is standing behind and off to the side of his brother holding a shotgun. Anthony points to his brother, "Yeah... well here's my counter offer, get off my property or my little brother will put a couple of slugs in you two losers."

Mo Fields takes the Glock that he has hidden behind his back, swings it around and fires in one motion shooting Frankie in the knee. Frankie Screams, "FUCK!" He collapses on the tile floor writhing in pain. Anthony Cordero doesn't flinch, his eyes narrow ever so slightly. The Hispanic maid comes running.

Fields looks at the maid and speaks in very measured tones, "Dame la escopeta, por favor." The maid picks up the shotgun and hands it to Mo Fields.

Anthony: "You two are dead, you know that don't you? Dead... D-E-A-D... Dead! You've fucked with the wrong guys."

Jesse: "Really? How do you figure?"

Anthony: "Ever heard of Nicky Fungo, we're related, and Nicky doesn't like people shooting his relatives."

Jesse takes out her iPhone and scrolls down looking for a number. She dials, "Hay, Nicky how's it hanging? Yeah, I'm back in sunny southern California doing business and shooting shit-heads. Nah not me, our friend did it. You know me Nicky; I'm a blade girl, no place to hide a firearm in tight jeans."

Jesse laughs. "Now is that any way to talk to a sweet young thing like me. So Nicky... Johnny asked me and our well-dressed friend to follow up on this Murphy business, led us to a couple of clowns that claim to be your 'mishpokhe,' the Cordero brothers. Seems they sold Murphy a dud; she wanted her money back, so they killed her. Is that so... his name's Luzzato. He's your nephew. He's their brother-in-law. In other words, you're not close. So you don't mind we mess them up a little and take the money. Fine with me, but you got to clear the percentage with Johnny. You want to speak to him?"

Jesse hands the phone to Anthony, "He wants to speak to you."

Anthony: "Nicky these two psychos shot Frankie! What do you mean, so what? Okay, okay, the money too, shit, that's not fair. Shit! All right already, I'll co-operate." He hands the phone back to Jesse.

Jesse: "Yeah, take care Nicky, next time I'm up in your neck of the woods, we'll split a plate of those all you can eat meatballs." Jesse disconnects and slides her phone back into the pocket of her jeans. She turns to Anthony, "Stop whining, we're letting you keep your share of the insurance money you got from the Argentinean outfit for killing Rebel Beast." Jesse pauses to think for a second. "So tell me... why unload the horse to someone in Argentina?"

Anthony: "We sold Rebel Beast's brother, Devil Beast, to a lawyer in Palermo, Buenos Aires and he had a client that was interested."

Jesse: "This Devil Beast had the same pedigree then?"

Anthony, "Yeah, but he was a runt. Nothing to look at, so we just turned him around for a quick buck."

Jesse: "So there's a Palermo in Argentina?"

Anthony: "Yeah, they got a big old fancy track down there, the Palermo Hippodrome."

 Jesse: "Interesting…"

Anthony: "Not that this chit-chat isn't pleasant and everything, but you cost me a million bucks, and my brother is bleeding all over the fucking floor."

Jesse: "Okay, don't get so excited. Here's what's going to happen now. You're going to give me the address and contact information for your brother-in-law in Sicily. You're going to take your dumb ass brother to your vet so he can fix him up. Then you're going to bring one million dollars in cash to the Shanghai Players Club and leave it with William, the manager, tell him it's for the blonde bitch with the blade. If you don't, we'll be back, and we won't be so friendly. Understood?" Anthony nods. "Oh and by the way, you might want to untie the cowboy in the guard booth, he might be having trouble breathing with all that duck tape we put on him."

GOOD EVENING MR. STONE

Part Two

8
Good Evening Mr. Stone

Jesse had no trouble stretching out her petite ex-jockey frame in the first class seats of the Boeing 747. She'd never been to Sicily or any place outside North America. It was exciting, and she looked forward to the experience. She suspected the Corderos had already contacted Luzzato with their tale of the crazy blonde bitch and the well-dressed triggerman that shot Frankie for no reason. She wasn't worried. Nicky Fungo also made a call and warned his nephew, "hands off the girl."

Before meeting Luzzato, she intended to go to the Monreale police to see if they could provide any details on Murphy's accident. She was due to land at the Palermo Punta Raisi Airport at 2:30 PM; she'd rent a car at the airport, drive out to Monreale, and check into the Baglio Conca D'Oro, a hundred-year-old paper mill that was converted into a luxury stone hotel. She'd take a nice long hot bath, have dinner, and get a fresh start in the morning.

After checking into her hotel, Jesse took a long, relaxing bath while running over in her mind just how she'd handle Luzzato. Feeling fresh and renewed, she headed down to grab something to eat. Like most North Americans, Jesse likes to eat, and luckily, her metabolism manages to burn off all the calories. Europeans don't just eat, they dine, and dinner is not a pit stop, it's an experience of artistic and epicurean creativity.

Go to any American mall and look around, the stores may be empty but the food court is jammed with people wolfing-down greasy Styrofoam containers full of imitation Chinese, Thai, Korean, and Greek slop that passes for food. In Europe even the street vendors are classier and the food better than the near-botulinal swill served on American street corners. Jesse has a big appetite and not just for food. Like most Americans, food, sex, danger, and life in general are things to consume rather than things to savor. Europeans are different, especially Italians.

Dinner is served under the stars in the courtyard of the ancient paper mill. Eating outside is not Jesse's first choice, but what the hell, when in Rome, or in this case Monreale. She had to admit it was romantic; too bad she had no time for such things. As far as available men were concerned, the appropriate offerings were limited. She couldn't have a regular relationship with just anybody. Imagine the conversations:

"How was your day, dear?"

"Oh just another boring day. Mo and I drove out to Anaheim at a hundred miles an hour to confront a couple of Sicilian shit-heads. We duck-taped some cowboy so he couldn't move and then Mo shot one of the assholes in the knee, but we did walk away with a pile of dough."

Nah, that wasn't going to work. She needed someone who is in the game. She loved Johnny, but he's like her father; there was Mo Fields who is handsome, connected, and knows the score. He's a definite possibility, but he has a daughter, Betty, and Jesse just didn't see herself as the mother type, but maybe. Maybe Mo would make a good match. She felt herself getting aroused. The food, the night air, and the excitement of meeting Luzzato all combined to get her juices flowing. She squirmed in her chair. She had to get a hold of herself. This is not a vacation; this is work. Luzzato is dangerous, and Nicky Fungo's protective threats aside, Santos Luzzato wouldn't hesitate to reserve a toe tag in the Monreale morgue right beside the late lamented peanut butter heiress.

In the past when she got this way she found herself in some upscale bar nursing a Jack Daniels till some lawyer-type hit on her; then a quick cab ride to the nearest five-star hotel; slam-bam-thank-you-Mac and back to work. That would usually cure her for a while, but Monreale is out of her comfort zone, way out, and she wasn't prepared to jump in the sack with some unknown Sicilian lothario.

She didn't even have her blade, too dangerous to take on the airplane. It made her feel naked and vulnerable. Maybe in the morning she'd find a local shop that sold what she needed. After all, aren't the Sicilians known for their blade work, or is that just a prejudicial stereotype? She made up her mind; first thing on the agenda is cutlery. The thought of arming herself seemed to signal her body that sex was currently not going to happen, but then she looked up.

"Excuse me Miss, but aren't you Jesse James, the jockey?" Jesse looks up. The handsome, rugged, forty-something, English ex-military-type is well dressed, well spoken, and polite, if not a bit formal. Jesse almost expected him to salute. His face is very familiar. He's Josephine Murphy's chauffeur, "My name is William Stone and I work for Mrs. Murphy, or at least I did before her death. I wonder if I can have a word."

Jesse points to a chair opposite. Stone sits. A waiter arrives and Jesse orders coffee and pastry for two. Stone's gaze is like his name, hard and unemotional. "Did your people kill Murphy?" Before Jesse can answer the waiter arrives with a carafe of coffee and the pastries. Jesse takes a big bite of stogliatella. She sits back in her chair letting the orange-flavored ricotta melt in her mouth. Her gaze locks on to Stone's eyes like a jet fighter pilot locking on to her target. She takes a sip of coffee. "This shit is good."

Stone takes a bite of his dessert. "The Italians know how to eat." Jesse and Stone sit quietly enjoying their dessert but their eyes never leave their targets. It's a non-aerial dog-fight performed without movement in the courtyard of a converted paper mill. Or perhaps it's the mating ritual of two deadly tarantulas.

Jesse takes another sip of coffee; her gaze never faltering, "You're ex English military." It's not a question.

Stone: "Paras, 1st Battalion-Special Forces."

Jesse: "I guess that makes you one tough son-of-a-bitch?"

Stone puts down his coffee, "Utrinque Paratus."

Jesse: "My Latin is a little rusty."

Stone: "Ready for Anything."

Jesse's stares, her eyes never leave her adversary, but her hand ever so slightly moves to the knife resting beside her dessert plate. "Then we have something in common. Oo-fucking-rah."

Stone speaks in measured tones. His voice is clear, precise, and firm, "Did your people have Murphy killed?"

Jesse remains calm on the outside but underneath she wants to rip this guys clothes off and fuck him right there in the middle of the courtyard, either that or, put the dessert knife in his carotid, "What makes you think that?" She runs her finger across the knife handle.

Stone's eyes move to Jesse's hand massaging the knife; then back to her eyes. "The Corderos are Luzzato's brother-in-laws; Luzzato is Nicky Fungo's nephew: Fungo is Johnny Luck's partner; you're Luck's protégé; and Murphy and you had a history: Medicine Hat, Danny O'Connor, and let's not forget Florida."

Jesse: "You seem to know a lot for a guy who just drives a car for a living."

Stone: "Utrinque Paratus, besides, I was more than Murphy's driver, I was her executive assistant. If you didn't have her killed why are you here?"

Jesse: "Because we think she was killed too, and if certain people think like you, that we had something to do with it, it could create complications."

Stone: "Governor Somersby?"

Jesse ignores the comment. "You find out anything?"

Stone: "The police are stonewalling. They claim it's an accident. She didn't know the road, and she was driving too fast. The road has a deadly reputation, etc., but why was she on that road at all? I worked out a safe route for her to take, and I checked out the car myself. Everything was perfect."

Jesse: "Perhaps we should pool our efforts. Work together. Either that or we might become enemies and that seems like a waste."

Stone: "Okay, that seems reasonable, how would you like to begin this partnership?"

Jesse: "Oh I don't know... let's have sex and see where that takes us."

GOOD MORNING MR. STONE

9
Good Morning Mr. Stone

Jesse wakes up in a tangle of white sheets. She stretches out to touch the now familiar body of her new English paratrooper partner, but he isn't there. Did she make a mistake? Last night was fun, more than fun really, a connection between two opposites that needed each other if for no other reason than neither trusted the other, or anyone else for that matter.

She was freelancing. She didn't know whether Johnny would approve of her new chauffeur pal; but he sent her alone, he trusted her judgment, so she figured she was free to do whatever she thought best, as long as the job got done. The trouble was, what was the job? Was it merely to find information? Was it to dust Luzzato? She didn't have Mo for backup, and Johnny gave her no specific instructions: just find out what the hell is going on, and make sure none of it comes back to bite us in the ass.

William Stone just might work out nicely in Mo's absence. It's not that she hadn't flown far from the nest before; there were those two years in Ontario, but even there she had backup, Zack Wei, the lawyer with the motorcycle gang history was her shadow. He saved her ass a few times, especially the time when the Sokolovs, a team of Russian-Israeli shooters were hired to take her out.

Still, she wasn't sure if Stone was friend or enemy, so for now he was frenemy with benefits. She'd feel a lot better once she had a blade, but where the hell was he? She sits up in bed to scan the room. Stone is sitting at a table dressed in his black Savile Row suit, white shirt, and black silk tie. The table is filled with silver serving dishes with fancy ornate covers keeping the food warm. "You're up, good, let's get to work."

Jesse: "Yeah, good morning to you too."

Stone pours himself a cup of coffee from a silver carafe. He holds it up for display. "Coffee? I took the liberty of ordering us room service. I figured you'd be hungry after last night. We can develop a plan while eating breakfast."

Jesse: "Yes General Sir, aye, aye."

Stone: "It's Major, not General, and aye, aye is Navy jargon. Coffee?" He holds up a ceramic mug with the hotel's logo emblazoned in gold.

Jesse gets out of bed. She's naked. She throws on a t-shirt and crosses the room to kiss Stone on the mouth. "Yes Major, sir. Coffee please." Jesse sits in the chair opposite Stone and together they devour two delicious servings of Eggs Benedict. Jesse finishes the last of the coffee, "Lets go the police station, maybe I can find some nice young policeman who's eager to impress an innocent naïve American who just wants to find out some information on the accident that killed her sweet widowed auntie." She says it a ridiculous southern California Valley Girl manner. "Think I can pull it off?"

Stone: "No!"

Jesse: "We'll see... but first I need some personal protection."

Stone: "From Luzzato or me?"

Jesse: "That remains to be seen."

Stone undoes the belt buckle on his pants and slips the belt out of his pants. He hands it to Jesse, "Will that do?" Jesse looks at the belt with a quizzical look on her face. Stone responds in kind. Jesse looks closer at the buckle and tugs on it; a four-inch stainless steel blade emerges from a hidden sheath sewn into the back of the leather. "Fucking aye, aye, Major!"

Stone: "I told you aye, aye, is Navy, I was Airborne Infantry."

Jesse gets up leans across the table knocking over a basket of rolls. She kisses Stone one more time. "Yes Sir, Major... better?"

Stone: "Better."

Jesse: "OO-fucking-rah!"

Stone: "That's US Marines."

Jesse ignores him. "I'm taking a shower." And she disappears into the bathroom.

Jesse and Stone finally make their way to the hotel parking lot. Jesse points to her Toyota, signaling that it's her renter. Stone shakes his head. "You ever drive in Italy?"

Jesse: "Sure... I drove up from Palermo."

Stone: "I'm driving, I don't want to see your pretty face splattered all over some Sicilian country road, besides, that piece of crap you rented is fine for LA, but this is Sicily." Jesse can't help but smile when she hears him call her pretty. Maybe Mo Fields isn't the only option after all. Stone points to the black Fiat 124 Spider Lusso, "That's our ride. It handles better on these mountain roads and it goes like stink." Jesse doesn't argue. They get into the sports car and head for the Carabinieri Monreale.

When they get there Jesse tells Stone to wait in the car. He objects. Jesse touches his hand, she's used to dealing with macho guys and knows how to handle them, but Stone is different. She's growing comfortable being with him, so she tones down her natural fuck-you approach. "Look, you tried it your way. Let me try it mine."

She doesn't wait for an answer; she just gets out of the car and heads for the front door.

Inside the police station she finds the equivalent of a desk sergeant that only speaks minimal English and her limited barrio Spanish somehow doesn't translate well. After a lot of ineffective flirting, she's told to write a letter to the Commissioner, or least that's what she thinks she was told. A young Monreale policeman stands off to one side snickering at the frustrated American trying to make sense out of the Sicilian bureaucrat. Aggravated with her failure, she turns to leave. She's annoyed. Stone will be disappointed. She doesn't like the idea of Stone thinking she screwed up, even though he didn't have any better success. It's not like her to give a damn.

As she walks towards the door, the young cop appears at her side. Jesse's hand instinctively goes to the new toy hidden in Stone's belt buckle. The cop speaks in broken English without turning his head in her direction, "I'll meet you in the car park. È troppo pericoloso qui. It's too dangerous in here." And he disappears through a doorway on the right. Maybe she caught a break or maybe this guy thinks he can score a date. The last thing she needs is some horny cop ready to jump her bones. She wonders what kind of jail time she'd get for carving up a Sicilian policeman. The vision of an Italian chain gang flashes in her head.

She makes her way to the parking lot. Stone spots her and starts the Fiat. She motions for him to wait. She hears a whistle and turns to see the young cop standing, smoking, half hidden from view by a police van. He motions for her to come over. Her hand goes to her belt. When she gets there, the cop moves back behind the police vehicle so they can't be seen.

"Signorina, I have what you want… information on the rich American lady. Nobody is going to tell you… è stata assassinata… she was murdered. The brake linings were cut. Mafioso big shot pays off the police. Nobody will talk to you."

Jesse: "So why are you telling me?"

He shrugs, "Sei carina, non voglio vederti ferito… You're bella. I don't want to see you hurt." Jesse reaches for her wallet to offer the young cop money but he shakes his head.

Cop: "No, per favore, stare attenti… No, please be careful." Jesse thanks him for the information. She heads back to the car just in time to see Stone getting in. "Where were you?"

Stone: "Watching your back."

Jesse: "I didn't see you."

Stone: "That's kind of the point."

Dinner With Santos

10
Dinner With Santos

Jesse arrived at the Ristorante Bacco at the appointed hour. When she told the maitre d' she was dining with Santos Luzzato his all ready solicitous manner turned to near sycophantic groveling, Jesse could have sworn he almost bowed. Instead of just handing her over to a waiter, he personally ushered her to Luzzato's table.

The dapper Sicilian stood as Jesse approached. She was surprised. He looked more like a Lamborghini salesman than a Cosa Nostra killer. He was expensively dressed, handsome, charming, and erudite. His manner was gracious like most Italians, that is until they feel you've crossed them, then brother, watch out for the knife in your back. As he greeted her with a kiss on each cheek, Jesse caught a fleeting glimpse of Stone scowling at a table for one in the corner. She smiled at the thought of him being jealous so soon. She caught herself quickly, this is a dangerous business, and romance would have to wait for a more appropriate time. But still, she couldn't help but like the idea that Stone looked pissed.

Dinner with Luzzato was a treat. Sirloin steaks, topped with a giant grilled Enoki mushroom and a side order of spaghetti alle vongole; for desert Luzzato insisted on ordering Tiramisu and coffee. The guy knew how to charm a woman. While sipping the best coffee she ever drank she realized she was falling into a trap. This is how it must have been with Murphy, but Jesse wasn't Murphy, and she wasn't falling for the Italian Don Juan shit, besides, hard-ass Stone was more her type. It was time to talk business.

Jesse figured there was no reason to play coy. Get all the cards on the table and see what the river turns up. "Why did you kill Murphy?"

Luzzato barely reacts, "My dear Jesse, I didn't kill anybody."

"I'll rephrase," says Jesse in her best Perry Mason imitation. "Why did you cut the brake linings on Murphy's car and send her down a mountain road at night guaranteeing she'd never make it back to Palermo alive?"

Luzzato pauses to absorb the impact of Jesse's understanding of the facts. "You've done your homework. I miei complimenti: my compliments."

"Santos, dinner was lovely, but we're both professionals, and things are what they are. I need straight answers to take back to my people."

Luzzato: "I really don't know what you want me to say, besides you could be wearing a wire. And it would be unseemly of me to pat you down in the middle of the restaurant."

Jesse: "Look… Murphy was no friend of mine. We had our share of disagreements, maybe not enough for me to send her down a mountain road in a car with no brakes, but sure… the old bat was a bitch. No love lost here, but her brother is Governor of California, and he's about to announce he's running for President. He holds the licensing power over some of our operations to which your Uncle is a partner. And your Uncle doesn't like to be put in the middle of a shit storm."

Luzzato doesn't respond right away. "I'm afraid you missing some key information that would put a different light on the situation."

Jesse: "Care to fill me in?"

Luzzato: "You're in over your head my dear. Why don't we drop the subject and order more coffee?" Luzzato signals the waiter to bring more coffee. Jesse's eyes go to Stone.

Jesse: "Okay I'll play along for now, but I will get to the bottom of this and if you fucked with my boss's best interests, even your Uncle won't be able to save your ass."

Luzzato pours Jesse another cup of coffee from a silver carafe, "Understood."

Jesse didn't figure she'd get a confession, but then, Luzzato didn't deny the charges either. His cryptic comments implied there was something else going on other than a murder to cover up the Rebel Beast insurance fraud. Perhaps the answer had something to do with the horses. "So the horse you sold Murphy, it had a brother?"

Luzzato: "Yes Devil Beast, a shabby looking animal, not much potential there. We unloaded it for a few bucks."

Jesse: "So I understand, to some Argentinean lawyer."

Luzzato: "No… I don't think so, I think it was someone local, but don't ask me who. It was a quick sale just to get rid of him. Like I said, no potential."

That was it. Jesse hit a nerve. Luzzato was lying and Jesse knew it. Truffatore already provided Jesse with the name of the Argentinean lawyer who handled both the Rebel Beast and Devil Beast transactions. It was a lead that Jesse could follow, and that meant a visit to the other Palermo. "I see… well thank you for dinner. I should be getting back to my hotel. The jet lag is finally catching up to me."

Luzzato waves a hand in the air and an underling almost magically appears beside the table, "I'll have Marco drive you. It's not safe for an attractive young woman alone at night on the street."

Jesse: "That's not necessary."

Luzzato: "I insist... really I do insist!"

Jesse's eyes glance over to Stone, who is throwing a wad of cash on the table to pay for his dinner. "Sure, if you insist, but first I have to go to the little girl's room." Jesse gets up from the table. Luzzato doesn't move. The niceties are obviously concluded. As Jesse heads for the washrooms, Marco takes her by the arm in a none-to-friendly manner. Stone casually heads in the same direction.

When they get to the bathrooms Marco follows Jesse into the ladies room. Marco still has Jesse by the arm. There are three women putting on makeup at the sinks. The women all look at Marco but don't say a word. Marco barks, "Esci! Esci adesso!" The women immediately stop what they're doing and hustle out the door. One of the stall toilets flushes. Marco still gripping Jesse by the arm kicks open the stall door. He grabs the woman who is trying to adjust her clothes and literally throws her at the entrance door, "Muovi il culo!" The woman scrambles through the door still trying to get her dress on straight. Marco points to the stall vacated by the terrified woman.

Jesse: "You like to watch, pervert?"

Marco doesn't answer. Maybe he doesn't speak English, or maybe he is a pervert, or maybe both are true. Marco gives Jesse a leering smile. Jesse looks Marco right in the eye as she unbuckles Stone's belt. Jesse and Marco are only a foot or so apart. Marco has one hand on his hip and the other stretched out holding the stall door open.

Jesse's eyes are locked onto Marco's. She gives him a smile and in one quick motion removes the four-inch stainless steel blade from the belt's hidden sheath. She stabs Marco in the hand holding the door open.

Marco screams, "CAZZO!"

Jesse doesn't let go of the blade. She puts every ounce of her one hundred and ten pounds behind nailing Marco to the bathroom stall door. She can feel the knife scratching the metal paint. Marco takes his free hand and grabs Jesse by the throat.

She can't breathe. She flails about gasping for air. Marco has her in a death grip. Then abruptly he lets go. An arm appears around Marco's neck. Stone has him in some kind of fancy military sleeper hold. Marco's eyes roll back into his head and he goes limp. Stone releases his hold and Marco falls to the tile floor in a heap. Jesse kicks Marco in the stomach. He doesn't react. Jesse bends down and removes the knife from Marco's hand. She wipes the blood from the blade on Marco's suit jacket. She looks at Stone. "Think you can teach me that move?"

Stone takes her by the hand, "Come on. Let's get the hell out of here."

THE OTHER PALERMO

11
The Other Palermo

Palermo is a barrio of Buenos Aires made up of smaller neighborhoods including the trendy artistic area of Palermo Soho where Luzzato's lawyer lives and works. There are alternatives histories as to how Palermo got its name, but both are connected to their Sicilian cousin. One theory has the area named after the Franciscan abbey of "Saint Benedict of Palermo" in Sicily. Saint Benedict is the patron saint of the Sicilian Palermo. Another theory has the neighborhood named after Juan Domingo Palermo, an Italian immigrant who purchased the land, now the barrio of Palermo, in the late sixteenth century shortly after Buenos Aires was founded.

The flight to Buenos Aires is uneventful. Jesse and Stone talk, sleep, relax, and generally get to know each other better. They land mid morning at the Ezelza International Airport located about twenty-two kilometers from the city center. The first thing they do when they land is collect their luggage and rent a car. As they leave the rental kiosk Stone notices a familiar face in the decorative mirrored wall hanging, behind the rental counter, it's the not so friendly face of Marco, Luzzato's man, complete with bandaged right hand. Stone nudges Jesse to look in the mirrored reflection.

Jesse: "Looks like we have company."

Stone: "Not the welcome kind. Let's check into the hotel and figure out a plan of action."

Jesse tends to be more of a free-wheeler than Stone. If she was going to work this scenario with her new companion, she realized she was going to have to get used to his organized military approach. Perhaps it was best. The situation was dangerous enough with Marco in hot pursuit; backup seemed to be a necessity, but was Marco here tailing Jesse, or was he here to clean house and eliminate the lawyer? Whatever the case, things were definitely escalating and fast.

Jesse and Stone drive directly to the luxury Alvear Palace Hotel in Recoleta, not far from the Hipodromo Argentino, Argentina's principal racetrack, home of the Gran Premio Nacional, the Argentine Derby. They check in to the hotel as Mr. and Mrs. Stone, no sense making it easy for Marco to trace Jesse. Stone wasn't involved in Murphy's meetings with Luzzato; and when he saved Jesse, he attacked from behind. All Marco knew was Jesse had backup, but who it is, would still be a mystery.

The Alvear is quite the place, elegant and expensive, a hostelry where the doormen wear black suits, top hats, and white gloves. It's a throwback to another era of plush red velvet and gold leaf furniture designed to evoke La Belle époque. It is the kind of place where you might share an elevator with Al Pacino, Antonio Banderas, or Sean Connery. It's that kind of place. It's a good thing Jesse brought her black American Express Card. Johnny wouldn't squawk about the cost, that wasn't his way, at least, not when it came to Jesse, and besides, if he did, she could afford it, there was always Daddy's little inheritance that still sat virtually untouched in the back of a truck in a suburban LA storage unit.

Juan Pedro Cervantes is the lawyer that handled all the transactions involving both Rebel Beast and Devil Beast. As Jesse and Stone sip coffee in the Alvear coffee shop, they discuss strategy. It is clear Cervantes is Luzzato's South American money guy. It's highly doubtful that he'd co-operate without some kind of leverage. Even then, knowing Luzzato's reputation, coercion might not be an effective tactic. They needed something more personal. A quick check of the phone book and a brief animated conversation with one of the waiters reveals that Cervantes' office and home are located beside one another in the colorful, bohemian barrio of Soho.

They drive the short distance to Soho. Jesse parks the car in front of a pink painted storefront that functions as a high-end art gallery. In the window, there's a Fernando Botero lithograph of an extremely large nude woman sprawled across a metal bed. Across the street are a series of Spanish inspired stone buildings, all with balconies, to which Stone dryly comments that occupants must come out at night to do their best Juan Peron imitations. The most elegant of these buildings is Cervantes office, a two-story, grey stone building with what looks like fifteen-foot high ceilings. Its multi-pillared ornate balcony is the most elaborate on the block. Beside it is a white-stucco building that the address indicates is Cervantes' home. Jesse enters the office building while Stone knocks on the front door of the home.

Jesse is told that Cervantes is at the Hipodromo Argentino to watch his horse, Devil Beast, run in the eighth race. Jesse phones Stone who tells her to enter the Cervantes home. The front door is open. Jesse enters the Cervantes residence. It is elaborately furnished in the over-the-top ostentatious fashion of someone who is determined to show you how rich and successful they are. Jesse's taste runs more to the Bauhaus styles of the early twentieth century than the more gaudy ornate show-off styles of an even earlier era. Jesse climbs the stairs to the second floor sitting room were Stone is casually sitting in a chair nibbling on a biscuit and sipping a cup of tea. Mrs. Maria Cervantes sits ashen and shaken while her sixteen-year-old daughter Margarita flirts with Stone. A Glock 18C Automatic 9mm pistol sits on the arm of the plush upholstered chair.

Jesse looks at Mrs. Cervantes and her teenage daughter. "I see you found some leverage."

Stone nods as he takes a bite of cookie. Jesse's eyes move to the Glock 9mm on the arm of the chair. "Nice piece, where'd you get it?"

Stone: "Mrs. Cervantes gave it to me… to be more precise, she tried to shoot me, but forgot to release the safety."

Jesse: "Doesn't seem to bother the kid any."

Stone: "You jealous?"

Jesse: "Not of her I'm not."

Stone: "What did you find out?"

Jesse: "Seems Papa has gone to the races. Devil Beast is running in the eighth at the Hipodromo. I'm thinking I'll meet him there and have a chat while you play house with the girls."

Stone: "Sounds like a plan. Want some cookies? They're not bad. Margarita baked them herself. Make some guy a lucky man."

Jesse: "Just remember I'm wearing your belt, so stick to the cookies and leave the Chiquita alone." Stone smiles and takes another bite of biscuit. Jesse spots a family photo of Juan Pedro, his wife and daughter in a silver frame. She takes the photograph out of the frame. She looks at Mrs. Cervantes, "Mind if I borrow this, I wouldn't want to hit-on the wrong guy?"

Mrs. Cervantes: "Qué estas diciendo? What means this 'hit-on the wrong guy'?" She starts to cry."

Stone: "No te preocupes. No significa nada. Don't worry, she's just joking." He turns to Jesse. "Get out of here before you cause any more trouble." Jesse leaves.

Jesse drives straight to the Hipodromo Argentino. She's surprised by what she sees. The entrance has a stone archway attached to a black wrought iron fence with matching stone pillars topped with huge brass flowerpots. Behind the gate is the main building built in 1908. It's an ornate Art Nouveau building designed by French architect Faure Dujarric. It seems more appropriate for a French government building filled with bureaucrats pushing paper than a racetrack crammed with South American punters eager to lose their pesos. It's Saturday, and the place is busy, but Jesse figures she can find Cervantes in one of the owners' boxes. She has time. The horses for the seventh race are just entering the track. She spots Cervantes in one of the boxes with some knockout twenty-year-old chippie whose cleavage is awe-inspiring.

She buys a program from one of the attendants and quickly turns to the eighth race. It's a claiming race. Devil Beast is a maiden; he hasn't won a damn thing, so the odds are high and the claiming potential low. Interesting. Jesse recognizes the con. She asks someone where to find the racing office. When she arrives, she is directed to the Racing Secretary who is in charge of filing the claims. She uses her limited Spanish to tell the man she wants to put a claim in on Devil Beast in the eighth race. She does a quick calculation from pesos to US dollars. It's about eleven thousand and change. The guy wants cash. She hands him her Black American Express card. It's done.

Maybe she just wasted eleven thousand dollars on a dud, but she has a feeling the fix is in, either that or the horse is better than everybody is telling her. She figures what the hell, in for a penny in for a pound; the current odds are 59:1. She goes to the betting wicket and puts down twenty-five hundred to win. If she's right, the winnings will more than pay for the horse, plus it just might supply a little extra pressure on Cervantes who obviously kept the horse for himself for some reason. The thought of owning her own horse made her smile. Maybe it didn't look like much, but somewhere under that mangy exterior surged the blood of Nearco, and that couldn't be a bad thing.

Jesse makes her way to Cervantes' box. She stands directly in front of Cervantes and his zuftig afternoon girlfriend.

Cervantes: "Quien diablos eres tu?"

Jesse: English Juan Pedro… my Spanish is spotty.

Cervantes: "Who the hell are you?"

Jesse: "I'm the girl who has a friend who's currently eating your daughter's cookies."

Cervantes: "Qué? Qué dijiste?"

Jesse: English Juan Pedro, English.

Cervantes: "What did you do to my daughter?"

Jesse: "We didn't do anything to her… Yet! So tell your friend to get lost."

Cervantes: "I don't believe you." Jesse shrugs. She takes out her phone and dials Stone. Stone picks up.

Jesse: "Let Papa talk to Mamacita." Jesse hands Cervantes the phone. Jesse can hear the frantic babbling on the other end of the line. Cervantes tells her in Spanish that everything will be all right. He's looking after it. He hands the phone back to Jesse and motions for the girlfriend to take a hike. She gives him a look that could kill. He reaches into his pocket and hands her a wad of cash. She stomps off in a huff boobs bouncing in rhythmic synchronization to the click, click of her six-inch do-me heels, much to the delight of the surrounding male spectators.

Cervantes: "What do you want? Money?"

Jesse: "Nah… I got money, although if you're offering, I'm accepting, but what I really want, actually demand, is information."

Cervantes: "What kind of information."

Jesse: "Why did Luzzato have Josephine Murphy killed?"

Cervantes: "I don't know what you're talking about. I'm a lawyer. I don't get involved in that kind of thing."

Jesse: "Okay, let's start with something a bit easier. You are Santos Luzzato's lawyer aren't you?"

Cervantes: "Yes… so what?"

Jesse: "So who owns the company that bought Rebel Beast?"

Cervantes: "I can't divulge that kind of client information. If it's money you want bet on Number Three in this next race. If you hurry, you can still make a bet. The odds have come down but they're still 53:1."

Jesse: "That's your horse, Devil Beast. You sure it's going to win?"

Cervantes: "It can't lose. The horse is lightning. Everybody looks at it and thinks, it's too small, too shabby... a loser."

Jesse: "Good to know, but I still need to know who owns that company. You want me to call my friend and tell him to eat as many of your daughter's cookies as he wants."

Cervantes: "You're a woman, how can you do such things?"

Jesse: "Stop whining for Christ's sake and tell me what I want to know." Jesse takes out her phone and starts to dial.

Cervantes: "All right, I'll tell you. Put the phone away." Jesse slips the phone back in her pocket. "Luzzatto and the Cordero brothers each own ten percent."

Jesse looks puzzled. "Who owns the rest?"

Cervantes: "Samuel Somersby, Governor of California."

Jesse: "You shitting me? Somersby is the one behind this whole goddamn thing? He had Rebel Beast killed for the insurance?"

Cervantes: "Yes... I guess that was the plan."

Jesse: "But why kill his sister?"

Cervantes: "I don't know. I just do what I'm told. She was causing a stink and Luzzato doesn't like complications. Maybe he did it on his own... or maybe Somersby wanted to get his hands on his sister's money. He's her only living relative, and he stands to inherit a lot of money, money he can use to run for President."

Jesse: "That's cold... his own sister."

Cervantes: "Luzzato finds out I talked, I'm as dead as that Murphy woman." Jesse remains silent. She doesn't know what to say. Cervantes keeps going on about releasing his wife and daughter but Jesse isn't listening.

After a long pause Jesse finally responds. "Shut the fuck up already, I'll tell my friend to let your family go. And don't worry about Luzzato, he got his share of the insurance money, that's all he cares about. Besides you work for us now. If he gives you any grief, tell him to speak to his Uncle Nicky and his Chinese pals." Jesse takes out her phone and dials Stone. "Okay it's done. I'll tell you in person, you won't be happy. And get the recipe for those cookies, they looked pretty good."

Cervantes: "You were really talking about cookies?"

Jesse replies with mock offense, "Jesus… what did you think I was talking about? What kind of girl do you think I am?"

Cervantes' face goes beet red. Jesse laughs. "Just messing with you Juan Pedro. You're way too serious. You got to lighten up. By the way, I need you to arrange something for me." Jesse takes one of her Hancock Racetrack business cards out of her pocket. She writes Avi Ledger's name and phone number on the back. Ledger is a trainer and an old friend of Jesse's. "That's me, Jesse James. The name on the back is my trainer. I want you to make the arrangements and have my horse sent to Avi as soon as possible." Cervantes seems to have calmed down. The eighth race is about to start.

Cervantes: "This is my race. You should have placed a bet. The three horse, he's mine, Desert Beast, doesn't look like much, but he can fly." Cervantes and Jesse watch the race and Devil Beast wins by three lengths. Cervantes is excited. He pulls out the tickets he had on the race and kisses them. He then turns to Jesse. "Your horse, you didn't tell me who it is?"

Jesse: "Oh yah… I claimed Devil Beast. I figured you had some scheme you were running. She hands Cervantes her winning ticket. Cash the ticket and use what you need including your fee to send Devil Beast to the States. You can wire me the balance. And if something happens to that horse before Avi signs for him, my friend and I will be back, and it won't be for the fucking cookies."

THE BOTERO

12
The Botero

Stone patiently waits to hear back from Jesse. Their next move depends on the information Jesse is able to extract from Juan Pedro Cervantes. Stone casually wanders over to the window, he pulls back the curtain a few inches and looks out. A car pulls into a parking spot across the street in front of the pink art gallery. The door to the car opens. Stone notices the bandaged right hand. It's Marco. Marco looks across the street in the direction of the Cervantes' residence as if checking the address. He scans the street looking for surveillance or bodyguards; smart, wealthy South Americans are vulnerable to kidnapping and they often have protection. Cervantes didn't feel the need; after all, he was Luzzato's man, and that seemed protection enough for the lawyer. He might change his mind by the end of the day.

Marco notices the art gallery and the Botero in the window. He stares at the lithograph for a long minute. He seems fascinated by the buxom come-hither nude. He enters the art gallery.

Stone turns from the window and looks at Mrs. Cervantes and her daughter. The teenager is prattling on in Spanish about some bullshit adolescent shit concerning how immature the boys are at school and how her tastes tend for the more mature male, men like Stone. Mrs. Cervantes tries in vain to shut her daughter up.

Stone speaks, "Silencio!" He looks at the mother. He's about to tell her to take her daughter into the bedroom, but he thinks better of it. "Come with me." Mrs. Cervantes starts to quiver and shake with fear, the daughter tries to calm her. Stone takes the two women into the bedroom and tells them to lie down on the bed beside one another. The mother is hysterical, crying, babbling in Spanish pleading for her life. The daughter is just excited. Stone spots a phone beside the bed. He grabs it and rips it out of the wall. Maria Cervantes is inconsolable.

The teenager looks at Stone, "Qué pasa con los teléfonos celulares?" She's offering the cell phones.

Stone nods, "Si, get the cell phones." The girl jumps off the bed and runs out of the room. She comes back holding two purses. She dumps the contents of the purses on the floor. Her mother is lying on the bed with her hands clasped together praying to Jesus for mercy, but Jesus isn't answering. Their only available savior is Major William Stone, retired. The girl hands Stone two iPhones, one white, the other rose gold. Stone sticks them in his pocket. The teenager smiles and jumps back on the bed. She attempts to calm her mother. Stone speaks directly to the teenager. Her mother is too distraught to comprehend

Stone's instructions. "Someone is coming to hurt you, but don't worry, I'll protect you. Stay here and be still. Try to keep your mother calm. Do you understand?" The girl nods.

Stone goes back into the sitting room. He phones Jesse as he carefully peers out the window scanning the street for Marco. Jesse answers: "I'm on my way back now with Juan Pedro. What's up?

Stone: "Marco is here."

Jesse: "Shit!"

Stone: "You better get here fast, it looks like trouble." Jesse hangs up and drops the phone into the car's cup holder. She jams her foot down on the accelerator making the renter lunge forward like Nearco turning for home. She weaves in and out of traffic in a frenzied race back to the Cervantes residence. Juan Pedro is white as a ghost, holding on to the armrest with one hand and the seat with his other. Jesse spots an opening; she guns the engine into the next gear. She narrowly misses a Volkswagen bug on one side and a Mini Cooper on the other, time is running out.

Stone keeps his eyes firmly on the front of the art gallery. Marco exits carrying a large brown paper wrapped package. Stone thinks, 'Jesus is this guy Italian or what? On his way to a murder, he stops off to buy a Botero lithograph.' Marco opens the trunk of the renter and puts his new purchase in the boot. He closes the trunk and crosses the street heading for the Cervantes front door.

Stone races down stairs and takes his position to the right of the front door with the Glock raised above his head ready to come down on Marco's head as he enters the Cervantes home. The door opens slowly and Marco peaks his head in through the front door. The Glock finds its mark, but the Sicilian has a hard head; he groans as he stumbles into the house. With Marco bent over, Stone grabs the back of his collar with his free hand and flings Marco headfirst into the staircase.

Marco collapses in a heap, blood oozing from the back of his head where the Glock hit its mark and from the front of his head where it greeted the staircase. He was down for the count, most assuredly with a concussion. Stone rushes up stairs to the bedroom, grabs the cord from the phone he ripped out of the wall, and tries to remove it, but it won't come loose. He takes it anyway with the phone attached. He orders Mrs. Cervantes and her daughter to come with him. They follow him to the top of the steps when the teenager stops and tells Stone to wait. She runs into the kitchen and brings back a twelve-inch Henckels cooking knife. She hands it to Stone. He cuts the cord free. He uses the cord to tie Marco's hands behind his back. Stone orders Mrs.

Cervantes and Margarita to grab Marco's legs while Stone grabs him under the arms. They not so gently drag him up the stairs and deposit him in a chintz chair in the middle of the sitting room. Stone goes into the bedroom and takes a pillowcase off one of the pillows and places it over Marco's head.

Stone is in good shape but Marco is heavier than he looks, Stone figures all that Sicilian pasta had to end up somewhere. Stone checks Marco's pockets. He takes his wallet, passport, and car keys. He sits down in his usual chair and waits for Jesse while Margarita makes more tea along with another plate full of homemade cookies. Mrs. Cervantes finally calms down. She thanks Stone for protecting her and her daughter. She apologizes for not understanding he was there to protect them. She can't stop hugging him and kissing his hand. She thanks Jesus and the Almighty himself for sending the handsome, brave Englishman who saved their lives. Stone doesn't bother to dissuade her from her misguided impression.

Jesse and Cervantes rush into the house quickly noticing the blood on the steps and obvious signs of a struggle. Jesse removes the blade from the belt Stone gave her. They climb the steps. When they enter the living room Stone is sitting on the couch between Mrs. Cervantes and Margarita. Mrs. Cervantes has a photo album spread across Stones knees and is babbling on about what's in the photographs. The coffee table is littered with three China teacups and the remains of a plate that once contained homemade cookies. Under the photo album Margarita's hand keeps moving to Stones' inner thigh despite his attempts to remove it, only Jesse notices. The scene of domestic bliss is shattered by Marco's moan from across the room.

Stone looks up. His eyes meet Jesse's. She looks pissed. He removes Margarita's hand from his inner thigh for the last time. Stone stands and approaches Jesse while Juan Pedro embraces his wife and daughter. Jesse gives Stone a hard look, "I see you had some fun."

Stone: "He didn't put up much of a fight. I got him as he was coming in the front door."

Jesse: "That's not exactly what I was referring to."

Stone: "What are you talking about... the kid? Please... don't be ridiculous."

Jesse didn't realize how attached she was becoming to the Englishman. She never thought of herself as the jealous type but this was different. He was different, and all of a sudden sharing him felt wrong. "Okay if you say so." She was obviously still perturbed, but Stone didn't understand why. Margarita was just a little girl with an infatuation for a dangerous tough guy, yet he couldn't resist a final jab.

Stone: "She does make great cookies, and I kind of enjoyed the photo album." Jesse gives him the stink eye. Stone ignores her, "So what are we going to do with Marco. He's probably got a concussion to match the hole you put in his hand."

Jesse shrugs. "Can he breathe under that thing?" referring to the pillowcase over Marco's head.

Stone: "I don't know, maybe. I didn't want him to see my face."

Jesse takes out her phone and calls Johnny Luck in LA. Better to have Luck call Nicky Fungo just in case he gets upset. Jesse tells Luck the situation. He tells Jesse to hold tight while he calls Nicky. Fifteen minutes later Luck calls back. Luck tells Jesse to get Marco in his car and drive him to a small medical clinic in Soho. Luzzato will take things from there. Marco is his responsibility. He also tells Jesse that Nicky warned Luzzato to back off any further moves against Jesse and the lawyer. To this point, nobody other than Jesse and the Cervantes' family were aware of Stone's involvement, and neither Jesse nor Stone figured they needed to know.

Stone and Juan Pedro get Marco into his car. Stone follows Jesse to the clinic where someone is all ready waiting for them. When they come out of the clinic Stone tells Jesse to wait a minute.

He goes to the trunk of Marco's rented car, opens it and removes the large brown paper wrapped package. "I know you're a little peeved at me, but the kid was just being a kid." He hands the package to Jesse.

Jesse: "What's this?"

Stone: "A peace offering... open it and see."

Jesse rips off the brown paper wrapper. "She's fat?"

Stone: "And naked... it's a Botero. All his stuff is like that. He's famous."

Jesse: "I like it, thanks. It looks expensive."

Stone takes Marco's wallet out of his pocket and rifles through it until he finds the invoice from the gallery. He looks at the price at the bottom of the receipt. "Yeah it is..." Stone then removes whatever money is in the wallet and sticks it in his pocket. He throws the wallet in a nearby garbage receptacle. Jesse smiles, "Don't I get a cut?"

Stone: "You got the Botero. Don't get greedy."

WHAT TO DO ABOUT LUZZATO?

Part Three

13
What To Do About Luzzato?

Jesse and Stone arrive back in LA early the next day. They kiss goodbye and each goes their separate ways with the promise of meeting for dinner. Even though Murphy is dead, Stone is still employed by her holding company. His duties as her chauffeur are over, but he still has his executive assistant responsibilities to fulfill, at least until her estate is settled.

Jesse heads to the Hancock to check in with her General Manager, Milton Goldstein. Milton is an old reliable family friend and her late father's accountant. Goldstein followed Jesse up to Canada to help her run the Crystal Beach operation, followed by a stint at the Woodbridge track, and now, both are back at the Hancock in Los Angeles. Johnny Luck and Milton Goldstein are Jesse's closest trusted associates, and both men would do anything for her.

After checking in with Milton to make sure everything is under control at the track, Jesse walks over to her office at the Shanghai Player's Club where she speaks to Johnny Luck about what she found out from Cervantes in Argentina. Governor Samuel Somersby was behind the death of Rebel Beast in order to collect the insurance money. It seems obvious that

Somersby is also the one that arranged for Luzzato to kill his sister. The motive for both the horse and Murphy murders is clear: money.

The insurance from the death of Rebel Beast is seed money to jumpstart Somersby's political campaign and to help finance his sister's murder. As Murphy's only living relative, Somersby stands to inherit the bulk of his sister's peanut butter fortune, a prize he can use to fund his run for President. The situation is tricky. Did Luzzato and Somersby do this on their own, or did Nicky Fungo make the arrangement? Johnny makes the call.

Johnny: "Nicky... it's Johnny."

Nicky: "What's up?"

Johnny: "I'm here with Jesse. She just got back."

Nicky: "Is there a problem?"

Johnny has to be careful discussing things over the phone. "Perhaps we should meet to discuss things."

Nicky: "I don't think I can get away right now."

Johnny: "Just tell me this... do you want us to back off this Palermo business?"

There is a pause on the other end of the line. Nicky is thinking. He knows his LA partners figure his nephew had Murphy killed, but he still doesn't know why. Luzzato claims he had nothing to do with Murphy's accident. He only went after Jesse because she was raising questions and sticking her nose in where it didn't belong.

Nicky finally answers: "Look… don't do anything. I'll catch the next plane out and see you tonight. Whatever he did, I didn't know about it, and if it's created a problem, I'll deal with it. You keep out of it."

Johnny: "Okay, we'll see you tonight. Come straight to the club and we'll have dinner. I'll set you up with a suite at the Towers." The two men say goodbye and hang-up. Johnny turns to Jesse, "He's coming in this evening. You can fill him in with what we know." Jesse nods okay.

She leaves Johnny's office and goes to her own next door. She phones Stone to tell him she can't make dinner, but he should come to her condo later in the evening. She spends most of the day returning phone calls and answering emails. She checks in with William, the Manager of the Shanghai Player's Club. William hands her a suitcase filled with the cash from the Corderos.

William: "I had it counted, it's all there."

Jesse zips open the suitcase and pulls out two stacks of bills; each packet is twenty-five thousand dollars. She hands them both to William, "One is for you, and the other is for Mo. Can you make sure he gets it?" William thanks Jesse for the spiff and tells her he'll drop the other stack off to the tailor personally, he needs some new suits, anyway. Jesse goes back to her office and counts out four-hundred-and-seventy-five thousand dollars and stacks it neatly in a box she got from the Club's dining room kitchen. The box will end up in her suburban storage locker along with her father's legacy. She takes the suitcase with the rest of the money to Johnny. She hands Johnny the suitcase, "This is for you and Nicky. It's from the Corderos."

Johnny zips open the edge of the suitcase and peeks in. "This should help ease the conversation this evening. You took your cut and something for Mo?"

Jesse nods. "Let's hope Luzzato went rogue with Somersby, and Nicky didn't pull this off behind our backs."

Johnny doesn't answer. If Nicky did this on his own, there would be consequences. LA is Hong Mian territory and Benson Yeung is the man in charge, the man Johnny Luck reports to. Nicky The Mushroom Fungo is a partner in the Hancock operation, but Buffalo is his town, not LA, and Somersby is California business.

When Jesse finishes with Johnny, she takes one of the Hancock golf carts that executives use to zip around the complex, and uses it to drive to shed row to see Avi Ledger. She wants to know if Cervantes made the arrangements to transport Devil Beast. Avi confirms transportation has been arranged and everything is set for when the horse arrives. Avi plans on a few light workouts before they really get down to business. Jesse tells Ledger about the horse's history and breeding. She tells him he looks like a shaggy runt, but the horse can run. Ledger's plan is to run Devil Beast in a minor race just to get him up to speed. He'll use The Pope, John Paul as the jockey and John Paul knows what to do: they'll just let the horse run easy and not show too much. Then they'll run him in the Golden State Derby Trial and see how he fairs. If he does well, they'll run him in the Golden State Derby.

Jesse decides that Avi should be the owner of record. She doesn't want any questions about her running horses at the track she's in charge of operating. Avi has been around long enough to know the score. He and Jesse are old pals going back to Jesse's short-lived but successful riding career.

Although Jesse has only been away less than ten days, it feels like she's been gone a month. It's good to be back in her element. She likes horses, better than most people, they're honest: some are smart, some are dumb, some are crazy, and some are sweethearts, but in the end, they are what they are. Horses haven't yet evolved to mask their real selves under a cloak of bullshit.

NICKY'S BACK IN TOWN

14
Nicky's Back In Town

Nicky arrives in town and heads straight to the Shanghai Player's Club. Johnny, Jesse, and Nicky have dinner avoiding the main topic, sticking to the mundane details of everyday Hancock business. They decide to have coffee and dessert in Johnny's office where they can have a serious private conversation. Nicky is aware of what happened in Sicily and Argentina, but he still doesn't know it was Somersby who had Rebel Beast killed. He thought his nephew was the one that ordered it. Nicky isn't happy about his nephews involvement. Luzzato pulled the Rebel Beast job without his okay, and without Johnny Luck's approval. Nicky claims his nephew admits to his involvement in the Rebel Beast insurance fraud, but denies arranging Murphy's accident. He insists he only went after Jesse because she was raising questions.

It's decided that when the truth finally emerges, as it always eventually does, it will be Nicky who decides Luzzato's fate. The nephew is really a side issue. Somersby is the real problem.

Governor Samuel Somersby is the Hancock consortium's political connection. It's Somersby that issued the casino license to the group's Native American partners. A Somersby run for President might appear to be a good thing, but it would increase the media focus on Somersby's career, decisions, and associations. That kind of scrutiny is not the kind of attention Johnny Luck or Nicky Fungo want. And then there's the potential Kennedy scenario: Robert Kennedy went after the mob after they helped elect his brother. When it comes to political associations, influence is good; high profile is bad.

Somersby appears to be getting too big for his britches. He's playing a dangerous game, making deals behind the consortium's back. Nicky agreed, despite his nephew's denials, that Somersby had his sister killed in order to get his hands on her money, and Luzzato arranged the wetwork.

Running for President is an expensive proposition and having money is a necessity. Big political contributors assume their investment will be rewarded if one of their own is in the White House. There is little Luck or Fungo could do to Somersby. He's too high profile, and he knows it. Nobody needs the heat a Somersby murder would generate, even if it looked like a Murphy-style accident.

Luzzato is Nicky's blood, and Nicky isn't prepared to okay a hit on him, even if he arranged the Murphy accident, that was on Somersby. Nicky would deal with his nephew in his own way. As far as the Cordero's were concerned, they were fair game, perhaps that would send a message to his nephew to mind his own Sicilian business and leave North American affairs to his uncle and his partners. Next time somebody approaches him with a deal like this, he better contact Nicky immediately. Luzzato's wife will not be happy with the sudden demise of her brothers, but someone has to pay the price. The decision is made; Mo gets another payday.

Johnny retrieves a handsome brown Cole Haan leather messenger bag from beside his desk and hands it to Nicky. "Your end of the Cordero business."

Nicky doesn't bother looking inside, "Thanks."

THE CORDEROS MUST PAY

15
The Corderos Must Pay

The black leather jacket, motorcycle helmet with blackout visor, jeans, and steel-toed boots are not Mo Field's standard style option. Only the thin, skintight black leather gloves are part of his usual operating wardrobe. Mo is accustomed to wearing fine, lightweight custom-made Zegna suits, accented by Turnbull & Asser ties, and Gucci loafers, but sometimes a job calls for something a bit different, and this was one of those occasions. It didn't matter if the Corderos saw his face, in a few minutes they wouldn't be able to identify him because they'd be dead, but the cowboy guard and Hispanic maid were innocents. He had no intention of doing them harm as long as they stayed out of his way. The farm probably had cameras, so a disguise of some sort was imperative, especially since he had already visited the place once before with Jesse. That made the whole motorcycle thing a necessity.

Mo brings the high-powered Suzuki Hayabusa 1300 cc motorcycle to a halt directly in front of the guardhouse. The bike will make for a perfect getaway vehicle if that eventuality becomes apparent. The cowboy looks up from the Victor Canning mystery he's reading. "Nice bike!"

Mo notices he still has his pistol strapped to his hip, Wyatt Earp style. Mo reaches behind him into the black leather messenger bag strapped to the back of the bike as if he's retrieving a package for delivery, but instead, he pulls out a TEC-DC9 semi-automatic. "Hand me your gun? Don't try to be a hero, you'll lose." The cowboy complies.

Mo sticks the pistol in the waistband of his jeans. "You have a car?" The cowboy nods. "Good," says Mo. "Get in your car and go home. Pack your stuff and disappear. Do you understand?" The cowboy nods again, but Mo's not finished. "If you go to the police, I'll find you and kill you. If you tell anybody about me, or who you think I am, I'll find you, your wife, your kids, and anyone else you hold dear, and I'll kill them all. And if for some reason I can't, my people will do it for me. Do you understand?" The cowboy nods one more time. "Say it out loud so I can hear you."

The cowboy stutters trying to get the words out… "Ya… yaa… yes sir."

Mo wants to make sure his message is heard loud and clear. He practically screams at the kid, "Again! God Damn It! Say it again so I can believe you mean it!"

The cowboy is completely rattled. He answers, in almost military fashion, "YES! SIR!"

Mo waves the TEC-DC9 in the air in the direction of the road and the Jeep parked on the shoulder. Mo assumes it's the kid's car. The cowboy takes off running towards the car as fast as he can. He fumbles for his keys. He opens the Jeep door, jumps in, starts the engine, and jams his foot down on the accelerator. The Jeep lunges forward, bucking like a wild bronco. The kid regains control. He takes off down the road at a high speed.

Mo opens the black wrought iron gate with the galloping thoroughbred handle. He leaves the gate wide open just in case a quick escape becomes necessary. He heads for the house. He drives down the long dirt road leading to the Corderos' resident-offices. He parks at the side of the house near a door. The door is open. He walks in. The Hispanic maid is folding laundry humming some Spanish pop song that can be heard endlessly on every Spanish-speaking radio station in Southern California. He points the TEC-DC9 in her direction. She turns to face him. She's nervous but retains her composure.

Mo: "Do you have a car?" She nods. "Are you legal?" She shakes her head. "Mexico?" She nods. "Leave now and don't come back." She nods and starts for the door. He stops her. "Is there a room with surveillance tapes, cintas de la cámara?

The maid nods, "Sí, la habitación al otro lado del pasillo." Mo motions towards the door. The maid leaves. Mo looks out into the hall. The coast is clear. He crosses the corridor and enters the camera room. Several monitors with different views of the property are attached to the wall. Mo can see that Anthony Cordero is sleeping on a chaise lounge beside the kidney shaped swimming pool behind the house. His brother Frankie is nowhere in sight.

Mo scans the room looking for surveillance tapes or discs. He spots an unmarked binder on the shelf. He takes it down and looks inside. Bingo! The binder contains discs each marked with dates that go back a year. Mo takes the binder out to the Suzuki and stuffs it in the black leather messenger bag strapped to the motorcycle. Now there's no record of his previous visit with Jesse. Anthony was a sitting duck, but what about his brother? Mo saw Pulp Fiction, and didn't want Frankie popping out of the crapper à la John Travolta, although it didn't turn out so well for him. Just in case, Mo does a quick tour of the one story ranch house including the bathrooms. Frankie wasn't home. This is a problem.

Mo thinks for a minute. He goes back into the kitchen and spots a Day Timer beside the phone. He checks it out. Printed neatly in clear block letters under today's date is the note: Frankie 3 o'clock – Crystal's. Who the hell is Crystal? Mo sees a business card crammed into the corner of the wall phone. He looks: Crystal's Palace of Massage Pleasure, Orangewood Ave, Crow

Village, Stanton, CA. As Mo is looking at the card, Anthony walks into the kitchen. He sees Mo, "Who the fuck are you?" Mo turns around and fires twice. POP! POP! Anthony is propelled backwards through the door into the hallway that leads to the kitchen. Mo goes out into the hall to check and make sure Anthony Cordero is dead. The TEC-DC9 did its job.

Mo leaves. He arrives at Crystal's Palace of Massage Pleasure fifteen minutes later. He parks his motorcycle in the alley behind the building. There are two semi-attractive, semi-clothed, massage girls standing, smoking on the steps leading to a red painted door with the word Crystal's scrawled on the paint in black, badly formed letters. The women spot Mo and then the TEC-DC9, they don't move. Mo reaches into his pocket and pulls out a wad of cash. He hands some of it to each girl. "There is more where that came from if you do what I tell you." They nod. "Is Frankie Cordero in there?"

The blonde hooker answers, "Yes, Room 6."

Mo: "Stay here and watch my bike. When the cops come, I wasn't here. You didn't see anything."

The Latino girl puts her hand on Mo's chest, "Cuánto más? How much more?"
Mo jams the TEC-DC9 up under the woman's chin. "Fucking be here when I come out." Mo

doesn't wait for an answer. He opens the red door and enters. There are random sounds of simulated pleasure emanating from each room. Mo walks down the narrow hall until he finds Room 6. He opens the door. A black massage girl is naked on top of Frankie riding him hard. Frankie is encouraging the hooker to work even harder, "Come on baby... come on baby..."

The woman turns to look at Mo. She stops gyrating. Mo raises one finger to signal the woman to be quiet. Frankie complains, "Why'd you stop?" Mo fires. POP! POP! He turns and leaves. He exits the red door. The hookers are still there. Mo goes down the steps and gets on his motorcycle. There's screaming coming from inside the building.

The Latino hooker yells, "Where's the rest of our money?" Mo sticks his hand in his pocket and takes out the rest of the cash and tosses it on the asphalt. He guns the engine and takes off as several of the other girls come running out of the building. The women see the money starting to scatter in the gentle summer breeze. It's every hooker for her self. A half a dozen nude and semi nude massage girls scrabble to retrieve the cash.

Frankie Cordero is dead. The message has been sent. Nothing happens in Southern California without Hong Mian consent, and that includes Governor Samuel Somersby and Nicky Fungo's nephew, Santos Luzzato.

THE SOMERSBY SUMMIT

16
The Somersby Summit

It's Trial Day at the Hancock, the run-up to the
Golden State Derby, and Devil Beast is entered.
The major competition is one of Josephine
Murphy's horses, Maximum Red, trained by Tony
Truffatore. Murphy may be dead, but life goes on,
and Truffatore is Murphy Stable's trainer until
someone tells him otherwise. Jesse and Avi
Ledger don't want to show all their cards by
pushing Devil Beast to his limit; besides, pushing
the horse too hard might burn him out for the big
money race. Two demanding races only three
weeks apart doesn't allow much time for the
horse to recuperate. If Devil Beast goes for broke
in the trial, it may not have anything left for the
Derby. Why show Truffatore what he's really up
against?

There are other considerations as well: if Devil
Beast wins the trial, it will lower the odds in the
Derby, and that would reduce the potential
payoff. The winner's share of the one million
dollar purse would provide a nice return on
Jesse's investment, but why waste an
opportunity to cash a pocket full of high value
tickets. It wasn't like Devil Beast was a perfect
specimen of equine beauty, an Adonis of horsey
pulchritude, prompting punters to bet on looks
and confirmation alone. There was nothing in the

horse's appearance that would signal the oversized heart that made him the horse to beat.

The plan is to see what Devil Beast will do on his own without jockey, John Paul, pushing him too hard. A fourth place finish would work out just fine, assuring that the odds in the Derby would be in Jesse's favor. If everything went as intended Jesse and Avi were in for a big payday. Of course when it comes to horse racing anything can happen, and it usually does.

Jesse wanted Stone to be in the box with her for the trial, but unfortunately he said he had some Murphy business to attend to back East. He promised to call her as soon as he gets back in town. The preliminary races were already underway.

Jesse sits in Luck's office making small talk with Governor Somersby and his trophy wife, Ellie, while Johnny Luck expertly mixes four Kentucky Buck's, a fruity concoction of chopped strawberries, lemon juice, simple syrup, bourbon, bitters, and ginger beer. Despite the superficial pretense of a relaxing day at the races, a definite tension filled the room, and it wasn't all because of Jesse's history with Somersby's much younger, beautiful wife.

It was Jesse that forced Ellie, an animal rights activist, to get involved with Somersby, but that was only supposed to be an information gathering honey trap, but the overstuffed politician jumped in with both feet, not to mention other more intimate body parts. Before Jesse and Johnny knew it, the fat politician and the pretty undercover mole were engaged.

Johnny hands Somersby his drink, "Perhaps it would be best if Ellie watched the races from your box while we talk." Somersby looks at Ellie who takes the hint. She gets up and leaves without a word. She knows all too well what goes on behind the scenes when you mix politics, horse racing, and dangerous people. Lessons she learned the hard way, not that she was complaining. After all, she is California's first lady, and her picture appears prominently and often in all the 'left coast' papers.

With Ellie gone, the conversation gets serious. Johnny drops his trim athletic frame into a red lacquer Chinese Chippendale, a match to the one occupied by Jesse. Somersby fills two-thirds of the three-seater upholstered tuxedo couch opposite. Luck has eclectic tastes. The Chinese Chippendales go very nicely with the modern sofa decorated in traditional Chinese patterned silk that matches the Chippendale seat cushions. Jesse is impatient; she doesn't want to miss Devil Beast run. She leans forward, looks Somersby in the eye, "Did you order Luzzato to kill your sister?"

Somersby laughs, "Are you crazy, why would I do that?"

Luck: "Running for President is expensive. It certainly wouldn't hurt to have a fortune in peanut butter stock in your back pocket... would it?"

Somersby: "Josephine and I weren't the closest, and sure I was involved with Luzzato on the Rebel Beast thing, but ordering a hit on my own sister... that's just ridiculous."

Jesse: "I don't believe you. You killed the bitch because you need her money."

Somersby: "Sure... Josephine was getting fed up with me hitting her up for campaign contributions, but shit... it was all tax deductible, so in the end she always came through."

Luck: "Fine, you say you didn't kill your sister. Maybe you did, maybe you didn't. The truth is we don't give a shit as long as it doesn't alter our relationship. Governor or President, you're our boy!"

Somersby: "You help me win, we're good."

Luck: "I don't think you understand. We're good whether you win or lose. How many votes do you think you'll get if we leak the story that you were involved in insurance fraud and three murders?"

Somersby: "Three murders? Who the hell else am I supposed to have killed?"

Jesse: "You killed your sister to get your hands on her money. You can deny it all you want. It's the only logical conclusion. And if we believe it, the voters will too."

Luck: "Then there is the matter of your other partners in the Rebel Beast business."

Somersby: "The Corderos? What about them?"

Jesse: "They're dead!"

Luck: "Who do you think the cops will target as their prime suspect when it becomes common knowledge that you, the Cordero brothers, and the Sicilian mob were partners in an insurance scam?"

Somersby: "But the Cordero brothers aren't dead."

Luck looks at his watch: "Yeah… I'm pretty sure they're dead by now."

Somersby: "I had nothing to do with any murders."

Jesse: "Even if you avoid going to jail, you won't be able to get elected dog catcher, let alone

President." Somersby is utterly confused. With all his political power, Johnny Luck and the Hong Mian still have him by the balls.

Luck: "One more thing. You don't make any arrangements with Nicky Fungo, his relatives, or anybody else without our permission. Southern California is Hong Mian territory."

Somersby: "So what the hell do you want?"

Luck: "Don't be so glum, Sammy. You continue to play ball with us, and nobody will ever find out what you did or didn't do. You'll pocket your sister's fortune, and with our help, you and sweet Ellie will be sitting pretty in a big White House. We want you in DC where you can do us the most good." Luck turns to Jesse, "What do you think Jesse? Would I'd make a worthy Commerce Secretary... maybe head of the FBI?"

Somersby: "Look, we've always worked together for our mutual benefit. I won't be dealing with Luzzato in the future, or anybody else without your approval. We're partners." Somersby lifts his hefty carcass off the couch, shakes Luck's hand, kisses Jesse on the cheek, and leaves to find his wife.

Luck turns to Jesse. "What do you think?"

Jesse: "Oh he'll play ball. He hasn't got a choice. The insurance thing alone would end his political

career, besides... he had his sister killed, no
doubt about it. Of course he's going to deny it.
Personally I don't care, I hated the bitch."

Johnny and Jesse head for the Director's Box
where they watch Maximum Red finish first with
Devil Beast an easy third.

TYING UP LOOSE ENDS

17
Tying Up Loose Ends

Stone lied; he's not back East looking after Murphy business; he's in Monreale, Sicily having a drink in the Osteria on Via Odigitria, the scene of Bestia's last hurrah. At least part of what he told Jesse is true: he's there to tie-up a couple of Murphy-related loose ends.

The tavern owner, Federico Falcone, is engaged in a heated conversation with one of his regulars. Stone's limited Italian catches just enough of the rapid fire animated conversation to determine that the bar owner is upset because his beloved trees were damaged by the young Vespa-riding toughs that show up for Santos Luzzato's semi-regular street races. Stone enjoys the comical Sicilian hysterics while he nurses his Vodka Collins waiting for nine o'clock, the time Santos Luzzato usually appears at his favorite dining establishment. In a few minutes he'd down the last of his drink and walk the short distance to the Ristorante Bacco where Luzzato dines at least twice a week. Hopefully tonight is the night he shows up.

A half hour later Stone walks into the Ristorante Bacco. He expertly scans the room spotting Luzzato at one table and Marco still with his bandaged hand sitting several tables away. The maitre d' greets Stone with practiced professional charm, "Buona sera, un tavolo per uno?"

Stone doesn't answer, he just points vaguely into the dining room as if he's there to meet someone. He walks up to Luzzato's table and takes a seat opposite the Sicilian mobster. Marco puts down his Negroni and walks over to Luzzato's table. Stone's hand moves in the direction of the 9mm Glock with the shortened Gemtech military silencer tucked neatly under his arm in the custom leather shoulder holster, but he stops when Luzzato waves Marco away.

Luzzato: "L'autista… the driver." A waiter approaches and pours Stone a glass of Perrier. He starts reciting the menu but Luzzato tells him to come back later.

Stone: "You're a creature of habit, same restaurant at least twice a week. Not a good idea for someone in your business."

Luzzato: "Have you been spying on me? Not a nice thing to do to your partner."

Stone: "I like to get to know my associates."

Luzzato: "This is not New York my friend, and besides, I have no enemies, at least none that are still alive. I'm just a businessman doing what businessmen do."

Stone: "If you say so. You tell your Uncle Nicky about me or our arrangement?"

Luzzato: "Why the hell would I do that? He finds out about us, he'll want a piece. As it stands your girlfriend and her pals all think Somersby is the one behind the operation."

Stone: "So nobody knows?"

Luzzato: "Nobody... not even Marco. You did quite a job on poor Marco. His hand will never be the same, and he still has headaches."

Stone: "What can I say, he's got a tough gig."

Luzzato: "Gig?"

Stone: "Job."

Luzzato pauses, rubs his chin, "So what's the final take?"

Stone: "They're reading the will on Friday."

Luzzato: "So why are you here?"

Stone knocks his linen napkin on the tile floor. He bends down to retrieve it; as he does, he removes the 9mm Glock with the Gemtech silencer from its holster. He covers the gun with the napkin and brings both up onto the table. The Glock is aimed directly at Luzzato's chest, center mass. He fires once, twice, three time in rapid succession. The silencer works like a dream, the muffled pop, pop, pop, is drowned out by the significant evening dinner chatter and restaurant bustle. The force of the impact drives Luzzato back in his chair, then forward face down on the table.

Stone jumps to his feet knocking over his chair. He shouts: "Aiuto! Attacco di cuore! Aiuto! Attacco di cuore!" Waiters, customers, and Marco all rush to the table to respond to the cries for help. Stone still has the Glock in his hand covered by the white linen napkin. He backs up as Marco tries to push his way through the crowd gathered around Luzzato. He's too late; Luzzato is dead. As Stone passes behind Marco, he expertly puts one bullet in the back of his head. Marco falls to the floor. In the confusion nobody notices. Their attention is centered on the dead local Mafioso, Santos Luzzato.

Stone heads for the fire exit at the back of the restaurant. He opens the door with the linen napkin. The alarm goes off signaling a fire. The customers in the restaurant all scramble for the front door not knowing what exactly is going on. There's nothing they could do for the two dead gangsters.

Stone hasn't touched anything in the restaurant. He's left no fingerprints. Mass confusion surrounds the building, everywhere but the back alley. Earlier in the day Stone stole a Vespa scooter, leaving it waiting in the alley behind the restaurant. He gets on the scooter and heads out of town making his way back to Palermo where he'll catch the red-eye to New York. In a couple of days he'll be back in Los Angeles for the reading of the will. The loose ends have been tied.

WHERE THERE'S A WILL, THERE'S A WAY

18
Where There's A Will, There's A Way

The LA Law Offices of McDonald, Singer, and Gold occupy the top two floors of the Exchange Tower in downtown Los Angeles. Leon Singer is just what you'd expect from a lawyer whose clients carried seven-figure and above balances in their checking accounts. Although no white shoes were evident in the Brooks Brothers' environment, it's clear the place is the definition of a white shoe law firm. It's the kind of place where Casual Fridays means Gucci loafers rather than Crockett & Jones Drummond Wingcap Brogues.

Singer is a handsome, maybe even dashing, fifty something solicitor with a shock of well-trained grey hair that silently states, 'if you have to ask, you can't afford it.' He sits like a judge at the end of an impressive burl oak boardroom table in his perfect custom pinstripe suit created by none other than Mo Fields in his Three Kings Custom Taylor Shop. The massive picture window that stretches from one end of the boardroom to the other provides the most dramatic, expansive view of the Los Angele's business district.

Sitting on one side of the massive boardroom table in the high-back brown leather chairs are Governor Samuel Somersby and his wife Ellie Lang Somersby. Sitting opposite are Tony Truffatore and Major William Stone (retired).

There is no sense contaminating the privileged elites occupying the Somersby side with the working stiffs that sit opposite. The anticlimactic distribution of the bulk of the estate is delayed as Singer drones on about small donations to Murphy's favorite charities.

Somersby smiles his practiced politician-smile at the plebeian legal participants that were about to share in some small way in his sister's bountiful assets. And why not, he thought: a few thousand here, and a few thousand there, wouldn't make much difference to the close to two billion dollars in peanut butter stock he expected to receive as Josephine Somersby Murphy's only living relative.

Singer: "… And to my trainer, Anthony Truffatore, I leave Murphy Stables LLC, including all horses, real estate, and assets owned by that company."

Somersby's broad smile fades just a little. 'Okay,' he thought. 'I get it. My only interest in horses is who's going to win the next race. Why do I need the headache and expense of operating a racing stable? Let Truffatore have it. In the larger scheme of things, it's peanuts, and not the big prize, the peanut butter stock.'

Singer: "… And to my brother, I leave a final campaign contribution of one hundred thousand dollars. As Governor and potentially as President he should be able to squirrel away a small fortune of his own without any more of my help that over the years has been substantial."

'What the fuck is this,' thinks Somersby, 'is the bitch stiffing me? Nah… can't be. She's just giving me a final dig. The big-ticket prize is still on the table and the only other person in the room, other than his wife, is the chauffeur. She couldn't help playing games, even in her final farewell to the world of the living.'

Singer: "… And to my faithful companion, secretary, and driver, Major William Stone, I leave all my remaining assets including my homes in Kentucky, Los Angeles, and Nice, plus my investment portfolio including all Murphy Peanut Butter stock that as of this date is worth one point seven billion dollars. That concludes my final will and testament." Singer looks up and smiles.

The color in Somersby's fat face drains. The smile is gone. His wife, Ellie laughs, the tears in her eyes betray the lack of amusement. Truffatore snorts his delight and turns to shake Stone's hand. Somersby stares at Stone with a mixture of envy and distaste. Stone blankly stares back. His expression is neither surprised nor pleased, like an officer who has just been told he's won a metal but at the cost of one of his men. Stone gets up and thanks Singer who says his secretary will be in touch. He leaves a very, very wealthy man.

RACE DAY AND NO STONE

19
Race Day And No Stone

The Golden State Derby is set for five o'clock but
Jesse is in no mood for a horserace. She stands in
shed row half-listening to Avi talk to The Pope,
John Paul, about race strategy, but she doesn't
hear a word. She's tried to get in touch with
Stone for two days without any luck. He didn't
even call after the reading of the will; he just
vanished into thin air.

Jesse is pissed. Where the hell is he, and why
didn't he tell her where he was going? He knew
today is a big day for her, getting the track ready
for the big event, with Devil Beast in a perfect
position to compete for the Derby win. Why
wasn't he here? Maybe he'd show up? Wishful
thinking. She knew better. She's acting like a
teenager. He was gone. Murphy's money changed
everything. Did she have it all wrong from the
start? Was Stone the one responsible for
Murphy's death, and for the troubling hit on
Nicky Fungo's nephew?

It made sense: get rid of the co-conspirators;
cover your tracks; disappear; it was the smart
move; it's exactly what she would do. Was he
capable of such a thing? In retrospect, why would
someone like Stone take a job with some old rich
broad? It didn't make sense. He was soldier, an

officer... a paratrooper for Christ sake; of course he was capable of killing.

Think about it, it all made sense. He was in the perfect position to get rid of her. He was Murphy's chauffeur and private secretary. Did he know about the will? He must have. He admitted to renting the car for her and even boasted about checking it out before she drove it. Was the Murphy-business he claimed he had to look after back East actually the murder of his partner Santos Luzzato? It's the old story: if you want to find the motive, follow the money, and the whole kit-and-caboodle found its way into the hands of Major William Stone (retired). She could accept all that, after all, she was no virgin; she pulled the plug herself on that asshole Gonzalez in Florida. She was scrambling to make sense of it all. She felt betrayed. She knew better, but Stone was different, it felt real, and not just on her part.

She'd heard the news about Stone's windfall from Truffatore, but nothing from Stone himself. She couldn't decide if what she was feeling was rejection, disappointment, or anger: now that Stone was stinking rich, did he not want her anymore, did he play her for a fool from the start?

When Nicky found out someone whacked his nephew, he went ballistic. His first reaction was to blame the Hong Mian. It took some real fancy footwork from Johnny and the intervention of the big fortune cookie himself, Benson Yeung, to calm Nicky's outrage and assure him that his West Coast partners had nothing to do with Luzzato's murder. No wonder Stone had been keeping his distance ever since they got back from Argentina. If Nicky ever found out Stone killed his nephew and she was involved with him, well… needless to say, that would not look good for her. Maybe Stone was trying to protect her.

She didn't care about Murphy; she didn't care if Stone killed her; and she definitely didn't care how much money he got from her estate. She had her own private stash neatly squirreled away in a storage locker in suburban LA. Her feelings for Stone ran deep, deeper than she cared to admit.

Meanwhile Avi and John Paul drone on about the race. Jesse realizes both men have stopped talking and are looking at her expecting her to say something.

Avi: "Jesse! Are you okay? Did you hear the plan?

Jesse: "Yah, sure. Whatever you say is good with me. Do what you gotta do, but make sure our horse wins. At least something should go right for a change." She turns and walks away without saying another word. Somehow without Stone the whole Devil Beast investment meant nothing.

As she makes her way back to her office, she's approached by one of the grooms, "Miss James, your friend gave me a note to give to you?"

Jesse: "My friend? Which friend?"

Groom: "The English gentleman, he gave me fifty bucks to make sure you got this note." The groom hands Jesse an envelope.

Jesse: "Did he say anything else?"

Groom: "No, just that it was important that you got this letter."

Jesse rips open the envelope and reads: "Dear Jesse, I'm sorry. Things were already in play before we met. Our timing just wasn't right. I will miss you. Love, WS." She understood the subtext, she understood why he had to disappear, but none of that mattered. His acknowledgement of his feelings somehow made it worse. She'd find the son of a bitch, no matter what it took. The first thing she'd do is pay a visit to that fancy-ass lawyer, and see if he could provide a lead, but first there is the matter of the Golden State Derby. As track director she had responsibilities and of course there's the race itself with Devil Beast primed to show his true colors.

When five o'clock rolls around, Jesse finds herself in the track executives' private box with Johnny Luck, Sid Goldstein, and a handful of Hancock

Casino executives. She'd rather be with Avi in the owner's box but she had no choice, she was the track Director and she was going to present the winner's trophy and check. Good thing Avi was the owner-of-record; if Devil Beast won, what was she supposed to do, present the check to herself? The whole situation is fucked up.

Johnny and Sid both know Devil Beast is really Jesse's horse, and each place substantial bets for themselves and Jesse through friendly third parties. They are excited for her, but Jesse's enthusiasm is gone. She misses Stone. She didn't realize how lonely she really was until Stone sat down across from her in the courtyard of that hundred-year-old converted mill in Monreale, Sicily demanding to know if she killed Murphy. It seemed silly now. Why did he bother? Maybe he was lonely too. Maybe their affair was nothing more than two enemy soldiers passing one another on a secluded road, tired of the isolation, fed-up with the strain, and craving human contact even if it's from the enemy. Sid and Johnny are the closest Jesse has to a family, and with Stone out of the picture; it looked like that was the way it was going to be for the foreseeable future.

Jesse watches, detached, as the horses burst out of the starting gate. Devil Beast comes out in good shape. He sits sixth as they enter the first turn. He holds that position taking it nice and easy as they round into the backstretch.

Truffatore's horse, Maximum Red, is sitting in third biding his time. Little Caesar is running first by half a length, but he isn't considered a threat. Maximum Red is the horse to beat, and Truffatore has him in great shape, and why not? The horse is his now.

As they hit the half-mile mark John Paul has Devil Beast tucked in behind the third horse where Johnson, Maximum Red's jockey, can't see him. Avi's strategy is smart. Jesse can't help herself, she's an ex-jockey, and her competitive juices are always close to the surface. She smacks her program hard against the rail as her other hand digs deep into Johnny Luck's shoulder.

She hears herself screech, "Run You Bastard! RUN!

Little Caesar is fading and Maximum Red is taking control. The horses pass the quarter pole and Jesse hears Johnny say something about the time is too fast. John Paul makes his move, he cuts to the outside making sure he doesn't get boxed in. One encouraging whack with the stick and Devil Beast knows what the do. The ugly duckling is gaining ground. Maximum Red is working hard. The pace is taking its toll, Maximum Red and Devil Beast might flame out, opening the door for one of the laggards, but not if Devil Beast has anything to say about it.

They pass the three-eighth pole and it's
Maximum Red by half a length over Devil Beast,
but Little Caesar is making a comeback. The son-
of-a-bitch was playing possum. The three horses
hit the eighth pole in a dead heat with Maximum
Red on the inside, Devil Beast in the center, and
Little Caesar on the outside. The horses are only
inches apart. Johnson takes a peek at John Paul.
He's worried. All three jockeys are using their
whips to maximum effect. Devil Beast is holding
his own. They hit the wire in a photo finish. Jesse
finds herself pounding Johnny Luck's shoulder
with her fist. Johnny grabs her wrist, "Take it
easy kid… you're killing me."

Jesse is exhausted. They wait, staring at the
flashing 'Photo Finish' on the tote board. Finally
the numbers come up: Number Five, Devil Beast
first, Number Seven, Maximum Red second, and
Number Four, Little Caesar, third. As Jesse makes
her way to the winner's circle to present the
trophy and check to Avi Ledger, she thinks, 'at
least I know a good horse when I see one; that's
more than I can say about my choice in men.'

NO STONE LEFT UNTURNED - LA

20
No Stone Left Unturned – LA

Jesse sits impatiently waiting in the lobby of the Law Offices of McDonald, Singer, and Gold. An attractive receptionist offers Jesse a coffee after which she busies herself answering the phone and making excuses why one lawyer or another is just too busy with really important shit to be bothered taking any calls. Jesse already wasted twenty minutes, and it was either barge into Leon Singer's office and cause a scene, or call in the heavy hitters.

She takes out her cell phone and calls Johnny Luck, "Johnny it's Jesse, I need your help. I've been waiting twenty minutes to see this lawyer. It feels like they're stonewalling me. That's right Leon Singer at McDonald, Singer, and Gold. We do business with them. They're the real estate shysters. Okay… Thanks."

The receptionist continues fielding calls, "Good morning, McDonald, Singer, and Gold, one moment please." Click. "Would you like to leave a message for Mr. Gold?" Click. "Good morning, McDonald, Singer, and Gold, one moment please." Click. "Good morning, McDonald, Singer, and Gold, one moment please." Click. "Would you like to leave a message for Mr. McDonald?" Click. "Good morning, McDonald, Singer, and Gold… Yes Mr. Luck, I'll put you right through."

One of the private secretaries comes out from the back and approaches Jesse. "Miss James?" Jesse nods. "Mr. Singer will see you now. Follow me, please?"

Jesse is led back into the same boardroom used for the reading of the will. She takes her seat at the burl oak table with her back to the window making sure the sun from the wall-to-ceiling glass wall overlooking downtown LA does not get in her eyes. Where you sit in a meeting can often be important depending on whom you are meeting, and it can sometimes mean the difference between life and death. Sitting facing the window with the wrong people could mean a bullet in the back of your head, but that wasn't something Jesse felt was relevant on the top floor of the Exchange Tower. That said, she still opted for the Wyatt Earp approach: sitting with her back to the window meant the sun would be in the lawyer's eyes and not hers. In Jesse's line of work you learn to seek out every advantage, even if the situation isn't the shootout at The O. K. Corral.

The handsome middle-aged lawyer comes in all smiles and business. "Good morning Miss James, how are you this lovely day." He looks around the room as if a bit disturbed. His secretary should have positioned Jesse facing the window. He would have to speak to her about that. He sits at the end of the table. Jesse notices him squinting just a little from the sun streaming in through the

curtain-less window. He strains to focus on
Jesse's face. He's uncomfortable, mission
accomplished.

"Mr. Luck called and said that it was important
that I speak with you as soon as possible. So…
what can I do for you?"

Jesse does her best to smile at the unctuous,
arrogant prick, "You can tell me where I can find
William Stone?"

"I imagine if Mr. Stone wanted you to find him, he
would have told you where he was going."

Jesse's hand instinctively moves toward the pearl
handled switchblade that is neatly tucked inside
her right boot. She stops. This was neither the
time nor the place for such a move. She'd learned
pressure can be applied in many ways, and
sometimes a few choice words were as good as a
blade to the jugular.

"I don't think you understand, exactly who I am."

"Well… you work for Mr. Luck in some capacity as
I understand it. And quite frankly that is the only
reason I even agreed to see you."

"As I understand it, you represent the Hancock
group in a number of real estate projects."

"That's correct."

"Well... I happen to be the Director of Operations
for the Hancock Racetrack and Vice President of
the Shanghai Players Club. Johnny Luck is my
surrogate father. I can tell you, he and Uncle
Benson would not be pleased to hear some
overpriced asshole with a hundred dollar haircut
gave me the fucking runaround. Now are you
going to tell me where I can find Stone, or do I
have to call Daddy?" Jesse really tried to hold her
temper, but then girls will be girls, especially
when confronted with a pompous jerk.

"No Miss James you don't have to call Mr. Luck.
The truth is I don't really know where he is."

"What can you tell me?"

"You understand Miss James, there is lawyer-
client privilege involved, so I'm afraid my hands
are tied."

"Your hands are tied are they? How would you
like to find your hands really tied as I drop you
into the La Brea Tar Pits?"

"There is no reason to get melodramatic Miss
James."

Jesse has had enough. Patience is not her
strongest virtue. She finds herself standing over
Singer with the pearl handle in her right hand.
Singer's eyes go to the pearl handle and back to

Jesse's face hovering menacingly over his. Singer raises a shaky hand trying unsuccessfully to create some space between Jesse and himself. He tries to be brave, but somehow the effort is feeble. "Do I have to call security?"

Jesse presses the button on the side of the pearl handle. Click. The shiny six-inch stainless steel snaps to attention. "Call them... by the time they get here it will be all over for you."

"Please Miss James, please take your seat, there is something I know that may help you."

Jesse puts away her blade but remains standing close to Singer. "Talk and talk fast. I've wasted enough time with you all ready."

"Mr. Stone arranged for a bank account at the Banque de Basel AG in Switzerland. Speak to Luis Briner. He's the manager. Perhaps he can help locate your Mr. Stone."

That afternoon Jesse was on a plane to New York where she catches a flight to the EuroAirport Basel Mulhouse Freiburg. By the following afternoon she found herself sitting across from Herr Briner in another expensively decorated boardroom.

NO STONE LEFT UNTURNED - BASEL

21
No Stone Left Unturned – Basel

This time the boardroom was as grey and sterile as a Swiss banker's reputation for hospitality. Of course that all changes if you land on their doorstep with a truckload of cash, any currency will do; not to worry if you're an ex-Nazi or deposed dictator; all are welcome as long as you bring vast quantities of marketable securities. Jesse learned to appreciate the elegance and simplicity of Bauhaus's black leather, glass, and chrome functionality. Her mentor, Johnny Luck, taught her well even though his eclectic tastes run more to the Chinese version of Art Déco, a style favored by his mentor, Benson Yeung, the Dragon Head of the Hong Mian.

Jesse had to smile. She remembered Johnny telling her the Bauhaus School was a bohemian enclave of artists, architects, and designers, many of whom were Jewish. Hitler couldn't wait to close the place down, but here decades later; she sat in the Bauhaus inspired Germanic capital of financial chicanery and money laundering.

Herr Briner is a tall thin, pinched-face specimen, tightly wrapped in a neatly fitting charcoal tailored suit adorned with a perfect Windsor-knotted tie of no particular color. The overall impression is grey. A look of near constipation passes for a smile. He is much younger than he appears despite the rimless glasses and touches of grey that etch his temples, all carefully designed to add gravitas to his still young years. His manner is brusque, irritated, and preoccupied as if he has much more important things to do, like bending his secretary over the desk to relieve his obvious frustrations. He sits across from Jesse in her jeans, Cuban-heal boots, white cotton oxford shirt open at the neck, and black leather windbreaker.

Jesse returns Herr Briner's forced politeness with a broad smile, "Am I keeping you from something more important, Herr Briner?"

Briner is polite, but aloof, "I do have a busy schedule today, but I am always available to meet an associate of Mr. Luck and Mr. Yeung."

Jesse: "Good, so let us not waste each other's time. I'm looking for William Stone. I understand, he or his money passed through your hands recently. So why don't you tell me where I can find him and I'll be out of your hair."

Briner: "You understand Fraulein James, institutions like ours do not give out that kind of information." Before Jesse can object, he raises a hand. "However, since you are someone of importance to Mr. Yeung and Mr. Luck, I believe I can be of some assistance." He reaches for the intercom in front of him and presses a button. "Bitte bringen Si emir die Datei 726397-01."

Within thirty seconds, a blonde Arian goddess struts into the boardroom with a thick file folder. Jesse pictures her bent over Briner's desk breathing hard, fogging up the glass and chrome Bauhaus classic, as Herr Briner rhythmically balances his sexual check book. Jesse winks at the secretary. The gesture isn't returned.

Briner opens the file folder and shuffles through the contents until he finds a document. Briner looks at Jesse. "Fraulein James, I'm afraid Mr. Stone may not be exactly who you think he is?"

Jesse: "What's that supposed to mean?"

Briner: "Fraulein James, this is highly unusual. We do not, under any circumstances, reveal this kind of private information, even for important clients like Mr. Yeung and Mr. Luck." Again, before Jesse can complain, Briner raises his hand. "However… this case is different. Mr. Stone, himself, anticipated that you might call inquiring after his whereabouts." He hands Jesse the document.

Jesse takes the paper and reads: 'Major Simon Hart, Chelsea Military Hospital and Retirement Home.' Jesse looks at Briner: "What is this supposed to be?"

Briner flippantly adds: "I afraid that's all I can offer you Fraulein James, unless you have a truckload of cash that needs to be invested."

Jesse: "Actually, now that you mention it, there is a substantial amount of US funds sitting in a rented storage facility that could use your expertise."

A MAJOR DISAPPOINTMENT

22
A Major Disappointment

After checking into her hotel Jesse takes the tube to the Chelsea Military Hospital and Retirement Home. The solemn red brick building with domed spire and multi-columned entrance is home to several hundred retired British servicemen. Major Simon Hart sits alone in a wheelchair staring out the window of the communal lounge. The room is populated by elderly men sitting reading, playing cards, or just staring into space, their minds pondering what might have been and wondering if the sacrifice they made was worth it.

Simon Hart is a seventy, maybe eighty, year-old gentleman with silver hair and a British military moustache that reminded Jesse of the one David Niven favored in those WWII war movies her father used to watch.

Jesse takes a seat opposite Major Hart. His steel blue eyes shift from the window to the pretty ex-jockey sitting across from him. He visibly brightens. There is almost a twinkle in his eyes as he scrutinizes his attractive female guest. Jesse sees him physically transform himself from an aging slumped bag of bones into what once must have been a dashing young military officer.

Jesse: "Major, I wonder if I can ask you some questions?"

Hart: "Do I know you my dear?"

Jesse: "No sir, but I was told you might know William Stone." Jesse can see the old man sag, but just for a moment. He quickly recovers and looks Jesse in the eye with what must have been a look that wilted many young soldiers under his command.

Hart: "If you're one of those American newspaper reporters, I have nothing to say."

Jesse: "No sir, I'm a friend of William's, and I'm trying to find out where he is, and what happened to him."

Hart gives Jesse a look of disbelief. "I may be old my dear and my memory is not what it used to be, but I am not suffering from dementia. What are you… twenty-five-years-old?"

Jesse: "I'm thirty Sir, and I apologize if I insulted you in some way, but William and I are friends, close friends, and he's disappeared without a trace and I need to find him. It's important."

Hart looks puzzled. "You're not a reporter?"

Jesse: "No Sir."

Hart: "If you want to find Major William Stone, you can find his headstone in the hospital's cemetery out back."

Jesse: "I don't understand. William is a young man. We were just in Sicily and Argentina together. He's in perfect shape. He can't be dead."

Hart: "I'm afraid you've been duped my dear, Major Stone died in 1982 in the Falkland's Conflict. He was my best friend and I miss him dearly. A lot of good men died back then, and for what: a windswept shit-hole populated by a bunch of sheep? Strategic value, that's what we were told. Major Stone was killed protecting that godforsaken rock in the south Atlantic. It's a goddamn shame, I tell you, a goddamn shame..." His voice tails off and his body slumps. His eyes move from Jesse back to the window. He's far away now, perhaps back in the Falkland Islands, perhaps with his friend, the real Major William Stone.

Jesse looks at Hart. A dreary sadness silently overwhelms her. She feels her eyes start to water. She feels the loss, not for Hart's Stone, but for her Stone: the Stone that never really existed. Was any of it true? Did he have no feelings for her whatsoever? Was it all bullshit?

Major William Stone is dead, so who is her William Stone. He sent her here to find out the truth, but not all of it. Why? Was he trying to disappoint her on purpose, stop her from searching for him. Well, that wasn't going to happen. She'd find him, but where? Maybe the answer could be found in Argentina. Maybe the Falkland reference was a clue, a hint, a breadcrumb, signaling her to head back to Palermo, Argentina.

NO STONE LEFT UNTURNED - PALERMO

23

No Stone Left Unturned – Palermo

On the plane from London to Rio, Jesse receives a text message from Johnny; he wants her back in LA as soon as possible. They have a racetrack and gambling operation to run; enough is enough. He gave her three days to find Stone, period, end of story. He expected her back where she belonged, making money for the Hong Mian, not chasing ghosts. She understood. Johnny was right. He wasn't trying to be a hard-ass. He just wanted her to move on. He wasn't worried about the business; he was worried about her. She'd always kept a distance between her romantic involvements and her personal feelings, but this time the guy got to her, and Johnny knew it. Okay three days. If she couldn't find Stone, or whatever his name is, in three days, she'd be on a plane for LA. She promised Johnny.

She really didn't know what she was doing. She was going to Argentina on a hunch. This whole mess started in Palermo, Sicily and maybe it would end in Palermo, Argentina. For some reason Palermo seemed to be the key. Obviously Stone wanted her to know the truth or at least part of it. Was he sending her a signal that he did really care, but that knowing him was dangerous and this was his way of protecting her. Perhaps the Falkland Islands clue wasn't a clue at all, just a weird coincidence, but experience taught her: there is no such thing. There is no way Stone is hiding on what the Argentineans claim as their Islas Malvinas and what the British claim is their Falkland Islands. What was Stone going to do, herd sheep with his billion-dollar numbered bank account?

She had no idea where to start. She'd only been to Argentina the one time. She didn't know anybody that could help her, or point her in the right direction. Her only contact in Argentina is Juan Pedro Cervantes, Luzzato's South American lawyer. At least it's a place to start. Jesse rents a car at the airport and drives directly to Soho and the Cervantes office and home. She finds the pink-painted gallery and parks in front. She sees they have another large Botero in the window. She likes it. It's of a rather fat horse with a rather chubby arm coming from off the image grabbing hold of the horse's reins. It would make a nice addition to her growing art collection but she had no time to waste on self-indulgence.

Jesse goes to Cervantes' office, but she's told he's out, probably banging that afternoon delight that was with him at the Hipodromo Argentino. She decides to go next store to his house. Maybe Mrs. Cervantes and her daughter have baked some more cookies. She realizes she hasn't eaten in twenty-four hours and she's hungry.

Juan Pedro comes home about an hour later. As he walks into the sitting room, he sees his wife chatting with Jesse. The coffee table is littered with the remains of a large plate of homemade cookies, a pot of tea, and an open bottle of red wine. The sight of Jesse unnerves Cervantes for a moment but he quickly recovers. Jesse immediately gets to the point. She asks Juan Pedro if he can help her find Stone.

Cervantes hesitates. "You understand Jesse I represent Mr. Stone. I helped him move some of his funds to various safe havens, and I look after some of his investments. He doesn't want to be found. He says, it's not safe, but he figured you'd show up here sooner or later. He's left you a note."

Jesse thinks to herself, 'another fucking note.' She's frustrated. She snaps at Cervantes, causing his wife to take hold of her hand. She calms down just a little. Cervantes goes to his desk and retrieves an envelope. He hands it to Jesse. She opens and reads:

"Dear Jesse - By now you know I am not William Stone but I doubt that that really matters much. Know this… I do love you and wish we could be together, but that would put you in great danger, and I couldn't live with myself if anything happened to you because of who I am, and what I've done. I know you probably don't care, but there are others who do. I am sorry. We weren't supposed to fall in love. Forever – WS.

P.S. If you're ever in over-your-head and need help, contact Cervantes. He knows how to contact me, but only if it's a real emergency."

Jesse looks a Cervantes, defeated, "Is it really that dangerous?"

Mrs. Cervantes squeezes Jesse's hand a little tighter. Cervantes sees Jesse is defeated, he tries to lighten the mood, "Don't worry Jesse, you're always getting into trouble, it won't be long before you really need his help." Mrs. Cervantes gives her husband a withering look. Jesse tries to smile but her heart isn't in it.

Cervantes tries to change the subject, "Jesse you remember Margarita, our daughter?" Jesse nods. "She works part time at the pink gallery across the street. There's a new owner, and he's trying to teach her the art business. You should go over and say hello, the new owner is very nice, and they have some wonderful new Boteros' and several are with horses."

Jesse smiles a genuine smile, but declines a gallery visit as she's expected back to work as soon as possible. The wild goose chase has to stop and now is as good a time as any. Jesse thanks Cervantes and his wife and leaves.

As she crosses the street to her car, she spots the large lithograph in the window of the pink gallery. It's a beautiful work of art and it would

look great beside the one Stone gave her. She
approaches the window and stares at the litho
for a long moment debating whether or not to go
in. She spots Margarita in the gallery talking to a
tall, slim athletic looking man with his back
turned toward the window. Margarita spots Jesse
looking in the window, smiles and waves. Jesse
smiles back. She waves and turns away. The new
gallery owner turns towards the window just as
Jesse pulls away from the curb on her way back
to the airport. Stone turns back to his
conversation with Margarita. Jesse will catch the
next flight to LA. The last stone has been turned.

The End

Author Biography

Jerry Bader is Senior Partner at MRPwebmedia.com, a media production company that specializes in Web video, audio, music, and sound design. Mr. Bader has written and produced dozens of video commercials for clients. Writing scripts and novels is a natural extension that grew out of the experience of creating attention-grabbing mini movies that focus on the core emotional motivator.

Over the years Mr. Bader has written over a hundred articles on marketing, and he's self-published marketing e-books, hybrid graphic novels, biographies, and a series of children's books. The Neo Noir Hybrid Graphic Novels are story concepts developed with the goal of having them turned into television series or feature films. There are currently ten screenplays, five of which have been self-published as hybrid graphic novels: *The Method, The Comeuppance, The Coffin Corner, Grist For The Mill* and *The Black Crane*.

He's also written *The Fixer* published by Rebel Seed Entertainment. It has consistently been in the top ten percent in several Amazon categories. *The Fixer* is based on the true-life story of a colorful horse racing character. The follow-up to *The Fixer* is the new book *Beating The System* that continues the story of the horse racing legend. Mr. Bader has also written *Organized Crime Queens, The Secret World of Female Gangsters, What's Your Poison? How Cocktails Got Their Names, Cowboys, Lawmen, and Outlaws, The Outlaw Rider, Dead End, Palermo,* and the soon to be released: *Stone Cold, The Aussie Switch,* and *Ballet Of Bullets.*

Mr. Bader has also written a series of children's books, ZaZa Books For Kids, that currently includes, *Two Dragons Named Shoe, The Town That Didn't Speak, The Criminal McBride, The Bad Puppeteer, Mr. Bumbershoot, The Umbrella Man, The Ninth Inning,* and *14 Ridiculous Tales of Sage Silliness.*

The Outlaw Rider

by Jerry Bader

Illustrated by Paola Ceccantoni

DEAD END

by Jerry Bader

Illustrated by Paola Ceccantoni

BEATING THE SYSTEM
By Jerry Bader
Illustrations by Paola Ceccantoni
Beat the odds. Beat the system. Survive!

NOIR I

JERRY BADER

THE GOLD CRICKET
THE BASTARD
CINE CITY
KILLER JAZZ

NOIR II
JERRY BADER
CULT
THE RED EMPEROR
THE REDHEAD RIP-OFF
THE INCIDENT REPORT